"Very Nice. . . ."

Taylor's lips trailed along her cheekbones, moving back to tease the corner of her mouth. "Why don't we try it again?"

"Don't you dare kiss me again!" B.J. ordered, struggling with a sudden desperation which surprised him into loosening his hold. "Do you engage in this type of unprofessional behavior with all the managers of your hotels?"

"My behavior at the moment has nothing whatsoever to do with your position as hotel manager. And you had better make up your mind whether you are being demure or provocative." His tone was mild, but B.J. saw that his eyes had darkened with temper. "By the way," he added, "no matter how you play it, I intend to win."

NORA ROBERTS
lives with her family in the beautiful Blue Ridge Mountain range of western Maryland. She is an ardent sportswoman and omnivorous reader, and has traveled the East Coast from Canada to Florida. She admits to being especially partial to spirited heroines and American settings, both of which are featured in her lively, contemporary romances.

Dear Reader:

I'd like to take this opportunity to thank you for all your support and encouragement of Silhouette Romances.

Many of you write in regularly, telling us what you like best about Silhouette, which authors are your favorites. This is a tremendous help to us as we strive to publish the best contemporary romances possible.

All the romances from Silhouette Books are for you, so enjoy this book and the many stories to come. I hope you'll continue to share your thoughts with us, and invite you to write to us at the address below:

Karen Solem
Editor-in-Chief
Silhouette Books
P.O. Box 769
New York, N.Y. 10019

NORA ROBERTS
From This Day

Silhouette Romance

Published by Silhouette Books New York

America's Publisher of Contemporary Romance

SILHOUETTE BOOKS, a Simon & Schuster Division of
GULF & WESTERN CORPORATION
1230 Avenue of the Americas, New York, N.Y. 10020

ISBN: 0-671-57199-0

First Silhouette Books printing January, 1983

10 9 8 7 6 5 4 3 2 1

Chapter One

Spring comes late to New England. Snow lingers in isolated patches. Trees begin their greening hesitantly, tiny closed buds of leaves against naked branches. Early blooms of color burst from the earth's womb. The air is fresh with promise.

B.J. tossed open her window with a flourish and welcomed the early breeze into her room. *Saturday,* she thought with a grin, and began to braid her long, wheat-colored hair. The Lakeside Inn was half-full, the summer season three weeks away, and if all followed her well-ordered plans, her duties as manager would be light for the duration of the weekend.

Her staff was loyal, though somewhat temperamental. Like a large family, they squabbled, sulked, teased and stuck together like mortar and brick when the need arose. And I, she mused with a rueful grin, am head counselor.

Pulling on faded jeans, B.J. did not pause to consider the incongruity of the title. A small, childlike woman reflected in her glass, curves disguised by casual attire, braids hanging impishly astride a heart shaped, elfin face with huge smoky eyes dominant. Her only large feature, they swamped the tip-tilted nose and cupid's bow mouth and were prone to smolder or sparkle with the fluctuations of her mood. After lacing dilapidated sneakers, she jogged from the room, intending to check on breakfast preparations before stealing an hour for a solitary walk.

The main staircase of the inn was wide and uncarpeted, connecting its four sprawling stories without curve or angle, as straight and sturdy as the building itself. She saw with satisfaction the lobby was both tidy and deserted. The curtains were drawn to welcome the sun, needlepoint pillows plumped, and a vase of fresh wildflowers adorned the high, well-polished registration desk. The clatter of cutlery carried from the dining room as she passed through the downstairs hall, and she heard, with a long suffering sigh, the running argument between her two waitresses.

"If you really like a man with small, pig eyes, you should be very happy."

B.J. watched Dot shrug her thin shoulders with the words as she rolled a place setting in white linen.

"Wally does not have pig eyes," Maggie insisted. "They're very intelligent. You're just jealous," she added with grim relish as she filled the sugar dispensers.

"Jealous? Ha! The day I'm jealous of a squinty-eyed little runt . . . Oh, hello, B.J."

"Good morning, Dot, Maggie. You rolled two spoons and a knife at that setting, Dot. I think a fork might be a nice touch."

Accompanied by her companion's snickers, Dot unrolled the linen. "Wally's taking me to a double feature at the drive-in tonight." Maggie's smug statement followed B.J. into the kitchen, and she allowed the door to swing shut on the ensuing retort.

Unlike the casual, old fashioned atmosphere of the remainder of the inn, the kitchen sparkled with twentieth century efficiency. Stainless steel glimmered everywhere in the oversized room, the huge stove attesting that the inn's main attraction was its menu. Cupboards and cabinets stood like veteran soldiers, walls and linoleum gleaming with fresh cleaning. B.J. smiled, pleased with the room's perfection and the drifting scent of coffee.

"Morning, Elsie." She received an absent mutter from the round woman working at a long, well-scrubbed counter. "If everything's under control, I'm going out for a couple of hours."

"Betty Jackson won't send any blackberry jelly."

"What? Well, for goodness sake why not?" Annoyed by the complication, B.J. plucked a fresh muffin from a basket and began to devour it. "Mr. Conners always asks for her jelly, and we're down to the last jar."

9

"She said if you couldn't be bothered to pay a lonely old woman a visit, she couldn't be bothered to part with any jelly."

"Lonely old woman?" B.J.'s exclamation was hampered by a mouthful of muffin. "She runs more news items through that house of hers than the Associated Press. Blast it, Elsie, I really need that jelly. I was too busy last week to go listen to the latest special bulletins."

"The new owner coming Monday got you worried?"

"Who's worried? I'm not worried." Scowling, she confiscated another muffin. "It's simply that as manager of the inn, I want everything to be in order."

"Eddie said you were muttering and slamming around your office after you got the letter saying he was coming."

"I was not . . . muttering. . . ." Moving to the refrigerator, B.J. poured a glass of juice and spoke to Elsie's wide back. "Taylor Reynolds has a perfect right to inspect his property. It's just, blast it, Elsie, it was all those vague comments about modernizing. Mr. Taylor Reynolds better keep his hands off the Lakeside Inn and play with his other hotels. We don't need to be modernized," she continued, rapidly working herself up into a temper. "We're perfectly fine just the way we are. There's not a thing wrong with us, we don't need anything." She finished by folding her arms across her chest and glaring at the absent Taylor Reynolds.

"Except blackberry jelly," Elsie said mildly. B.J. blinked and brought herself back to the present.

"Oh, all right," she muttered and stalked towards the door. "I'll go get it. But if she tells me one more time that Howard Beall is a fine boy and good husband material, I'll scream. Right there in her living room with the doilies and chintz, I'll scream!"

Leaving this dire threat hanging in the air, B.J. stepped out into the soothing yellow sunlight.

"Blackberry jelly," she mumbled as she hopped on a battered red bike. "New owners with fancy notions. . . ." Lifting her face to the sky, she tossed a pigtail behind her shoulder.

Peddling down the maple lined drive, quicksilver temper ebbed, her resilient spirits were lifted with the beauty of the day. The valley was stirring with life. Small clusters of fragile violets and red clover dotted the rolling meadows. Lines of fresh laundry waved in the early breeze. The boundary of mountains was topped by a winter's coat, not yet the soft, lush green it would be in a month's time, but patched with stark black trees and the intermittent color of pines. Clouds scudded thin and white across the sky, chased by the teasing wind which whispered of spring and fresh blossoms.

Good humor restored, B.J. arrived in town with pink cheeks and a smile, waving to familiar faces along the route to Betty Jackson's jelly. It was a small town with tidy lawns, picket fences and old, well-kept homes. The dormers and gables were typical of New England. Nestled like a contented cat in the rolling valley, bordered by high forested mountains to the east and the brilliant shimmer of Lake Champlain to the west, Lakeside remained serene and untouched by big city bustle. Having been raised on its outskirts had not dulled its magic for B.J.: she felt, as always when entering its limits, a gratitude that somewhere life remained simple.

Parking her bike in front of a small, green-shuttered house, B.J. swung through the gate and prepared to negotiate for her jelly supply.

"Well, B.J., what a surprise." Betty opened the door and patted her grey permanent. "I thought you'd gone back to New York."

"Things have been a bit hectic at the inn," she returned, striving for the proper humility.

"The new owner." Betty nodded with a fortune teller's wisdom and gestured B.J. inside. "I hear he wants to spruce things up."

Resigned that Betty Jackson's communications system was infallible, B.J. settled herself in the small living room.

"You know Tom Myers is adding another room to his house." Brushing off the seat of an over-stuffed chair, Betty shifted her ample posterior and sat. "Seems Lois is in the family way again." She clucked her tongue over the Myers' profligacy. "Three babies in four years. But you like little ones, don't you, B.J.?"

"I've always been fond of children, Miss Jackson," B.J. acknowledged, wondering how to turn the conversation toward preserves.

"My nephew, Howard, just loves children."

B.J. braced herself not to scream and met the bland smile, calmly. "We've a couple at the inn now. Children do love to eat." Pleased with the maneuver, she pressed on. "They've simply devoured your jellies. I'm down to my last jar.

Nobody has the touch you do with jellies, Miss Jackson; you'd put the big manufacturers out of business if you opened your own line."

"It's all in the timing." Betty preened under the praise, and B.J. tasted the hint of victory.

"I'd just have to close down if you didn't keep me supplied." Grey eyes fluttered ingenuously. "Mr. Conners would be crushed if I had to serve him store-bought goods. He simply raves about your blackberry jelly. *Ambrosia,*" she added, relishing the word. "He says it's *ambrosia.*"

"*Ambrosia.*" Betty nodded in self-satisfied agreement.

Ten minutes later, B.J. placed a box of a dozen jars of jelly in the basket of her bike and waved a cheerful goodbye.

"I came, I saw, I conquered," she told the sky with audacious pride. "And I did not scream."

"Hey, B.J.!"

She twisted her head at the sound of her name, waving to the group playing sand lot ball as she peddled to the edge of the field. "What's the score?" she asked the young boy who ran to her bike.

"Five to four. Junior's team's winning."

She glanced over to where Junior stood, tall and gangly on the pitcher's mound, tossing a ball in his glove and grinning.

"Little squirt," she mumbled with reluctant affection. "Let me pinch hit once." Confiscating the boy's battered cap, she secured it over her pigtails and walked onto the field.

"You gonna play, B.J.?" Suddenly surrounded by young bodies and adolescent faces, B.J. lifted a bat and tested it.

"For a minute. I have to get back."

Junior approached, hands on hips, and grinned down from his advantage of three inches. "Wanna bet I strike you out?"

She spared him a brief glance and swung the bat to her shoulder. "I don't want to take your money."

"If I strike you out," he yanked a pigtail with fifteen-year-old audacity, "you gotta kiss me."

"Get on the mound, you apprentice lecher, and come back in ten years."

His grin remained unabashed, as B.J. watched, stifling a smile as he sauntered into position. He squinted, nodded, wound up and pitched. B.J. swung a full circle.

"Strike one!"

She turned and scowled at Wilbur Hayes who stood as umpire. Stepping up to the plate again, the cheers and taunts grew in volume. She stuck out her tongue at Junior's wink.

"Strike two!" Wilbur announced as she watched the pitch sail by.

"Strike?" Turning, she placed her hands on her hips. "You're crazy, that was chin high. I'm going to tell your mother you need glasses."

"Strike two," Wilbur repeated and frowned with adolescent ferocity.

Muttering, B.J. stepped again into the batter's box.

"You might as well put the bat down," Junior shouted, cradling the ball in the mitt. "You're not even coming close to this one."

"Take a good look at the ball, Junior, 'cause it's the last time you'll see it." Shifting the hat lower on her head, B.J. clutched the bat. "It's going clear to New York."

She connected with a solid crack of bat and watched the ball begin its sail before she darted around the bases. Running full steam, head down, she heard the shouts and cheers to slide as she rounded third. Scott Temple crouched at the plate, mitt opened for reception, as she threw herself down, sliding into home in a cloud of dust and frenzied shouts.

"You're out!"

"Out!" Scrambling to her feet, she met Wilbur's bland blue stare, eye to eye and nose to nose. "Out, you little squirt, I was safe by a mile. I'm going to buy you some binoculars."

"Out," he repeated with great dignity, and folded his arms.

"What we need here is an umpire with two working eyes." She turned to her crowd of supporters and threw out her hands. "I demand a second opinion."

"You were out."

Spinning at the unfamiliar voice, B.J. frowned up at the stranger. He stood leaning on the backstop, a small lift to his well-formed mouth and amusement shining from his dark brown eyes. He pushed a lock of curling black hair from his brow and straightened a long, lean frame.

"You should have been content with a triple."

"I was safe," she retorted, rubbing more dirt on her nose. "Absolutely safe."

"Out," Wilbur repeated.

B.J. sent him a withering glance before turning back to the man who approached the heated debate between teams. She studied him with a mixture of resentment and curiosity.

His features were well defined, sculptured with planes and angles, the skin bronzed and smooth, the faintest hint of red in his dark hair where the sun caught it. She saw that though his buff-colored suit was casual, it was obviously well tailored and expensive. His teasing smile widened at her critical survey, and her resentment deepened.

"I've got to get back," she announced, brushing at her jeans. "And don't think I'm not going to mention an eye exam to your mother," she added, giving Wilbur a final glare.

"Hey, kid." She straddled her bike and looked around idly, then smiled as she realized the man had grouped her with the teenagers. Restraining her smile, she looked up with what she hoped was the insolence of youth.

"Yeah?"

"How far is it to the Lakeside Inn?"

"Look, mister, my mother told me not to talk to strange men."

"Very commendable. I'm not offering you candy and a ride."

"Well." She frowned as if debating pros and cons. "O.K. It's about three miles up the road." Making her gesture vague, she finished with the obligatory codicil. "You can't miss it."

He gave a long stare into her wide grey eyes, then shook his head. "That's a big help. Thanks."

"Any time." She watched him wander toward a silver-blue Mercedes and, unable to prevent herself, called after him. "And I was safe.

Absolutely safe." Tossing the borrowed hat back to its owner, B.J. cut across the meadow and headed toward the inn.

The four stories of red brick, with their gabled roof and neat shutters, loomed ahead of her. Pedaling up the wide, curving drive, she noted with satisfaction that the short cut had brought her ahead of the Mercedes.

I wonder if he's looking for a room, she thought. Parking her bike, she hauled out her treasure of jellies from the basket. Maybe he's a salesman. No, she contradicted her own thoughts, *that was no salesman*. Well, if he wants a room, we'll oblige him, even if he is an interfering busybody with bad eyes.

"Good morning." B.J. smiled at the newly-weds who strolled across the lawn.

"Oh, good morning, Miss Clark. We're going for a walk by the lake," the groom answered politely.

"It's a lovely day for it," B.J. acknowledged, parking her bike by the entrance. She entered the small lobby, and moving behind the front desk, set down the crate of jelly and reached for the morning mail. Seeing a personal letter from her grandmother, she opened it and began to read with pleasure.

"Get around, don't you?"

Her absorption was rudely broken. Dropping the letter, she lifted her elbows from the counter and stared into dark brown eyes. "I took a short cut." Unwilling to be outmatched by his height or faultless attire, she straightened and lifted her chin. "May I help you?"

"I doubt it, unless you can tell me where to find the manager."

His dismissive tone fueled her annoyance. She struggled to remember her job and remain pleasant. "Is there some problem? There's a room available if you require one."

"Be a good girl and run along." His tone was patronizing. "And fetch the manager for me while you're about it. I'd like to see him."

Drawing herself to her full height she crossed her arms over her chest. "You're looking at her."

His dark brows rose in speculation as his eyes swept over her incredulously. "Do you manage the inn after school and on Saturdays?" he asked sarcastically.

B.J. flushed with anger. "I have been managing the Lakeside Inn for nearly four years. If there's a problem, I shall be delighted to take it up with you here, or in my office. If you require a room," she gestured toward the open register, "we'll be more than happy to oblige you."

"B.J. Clark?" he asked with a deepening frown.

"That's correct."

With a nod, he lifted a pen and signed the register. "I'm sure you'll understand," he began, raising his eyes again in fresh study. "Your morning activity on the baseball diamond and your rather juvenile appearance are deceptive."

"I had the morning free," she said crisply, "and my appearance in no way reflects on the inn's quality. I'm sure you'll see that for yourself during your stay, Mr. . . . ." Turning the register to face her, B.J.'s stomach lurched.

"Reynolds," he supplied, smiling at her astonished expression. "Taylor Reynolds."

Struggling for composure, B.J. lifted her face and assumed a businesslike veneer. "I'm afraid we weren't expecting you until Monday, Mr. Reynolds."

"I changed my plans," he countered, dropping the pen back in its holder.

"Yes, well . . . Welcome to Lakeside Inn," she said belatedly and flicked a pigtail behind her back.

"Thank you. I'll require an office during my stay. Can you arrange it?"

"Our office space is limited, Mr. Reynolds." Cursing Betty Jackson's blackberry jelly, she pulled down the key to the inn's best room and rounded the desk. "However, if you don't mind sharing mine, I'm sure you'll find it adequate."

"Let's take a look. I want to see the books and records anyway."

"Of course," she agreed, gritting her teeth at the stranger's hold over her inn. "If you'll just come with me."

"B.J., B.J." She watched with an inward shudder as Eddie hurtled down the stairs and into the lobby. His glasses were slipping down his nose, his brown hair was flopping around his ears.

"B.J.," he said again, breathless, "Mrs. Pierce-Lowell's T.V. went out right in the middle of her cartoons."

"Oh, blast. Take mine in to her and call Max for the repair."

"He's away for the weekend," Eddie reminded her.

"All right, I'll survive." Giving his shoulder an encouraging pat, she guided him to the door. "Leave me a memo to call him Monday and get mine into her before she misses Bugs Bunny." Feeling the new owner's penetrating stare in the back of her head, B.J. explained apologetically. "I'm sorry, Eddie has a tendency toward the dramatic, and Mrs. Pierce-Lowell is addicted to Saturday morning cartoons. She's one of our regulars, and we make it a policy to provide our guests with what pleases them."

"I see," he replied, but she could find nothing in his expression to indicate that he did.

Moving quickly to the back of the first floor, B.J. opened the door to her office and gestured Taylor inside. "It's not very big," she began as he surveyed the small room with desk and file cabinets and bulletin board, "but I'm sure we can arrange it to suit your needs for the few days you will be here."

"Two weeks" he stated firmly. He strolled across the room, picking up a bronzed paperweight of a grinning turtle.

"Two weeks?" she repeated, and the alarm in her voice caused him to turn towards her.

"That's right, Miss Clark. Is that a problem?"

"No, no, of course not." Finding his direct stare unnerving, she lowered her eyes to the clutter on her desk.

"Do you play ball every Saturday, Miss Clark?" He perched on the edge of the desk. Looking up, B.J. found her face only inches from his.

"No, certainly not," she answered with dignity. "I simply happened to be passing by, and—"

"A very courageous slide," he commented, shocking her by running a finger down her cheek. "And your face proves it."

Somewhat dazed, she glanced at the dust on his finger. "I was safe," she said in defense against a ridiculously speeding pulse. "Wilbur needs an optometrist."

"I wonder if you manage the inn with the same tenacity with which you play ball." He smiled, his eyes very intent on hers. "We'll have a look at the books this afternoon."

"I'm sure you'll find everything in order," she said stiffly. The effect was somewhat spoiled as she backed into a file cabinet. "The inn runs very smoothly, and as you know, makes a nice profit." She continued struggling to maintain her dignity.

"With a few changes, it should make a great deal more."

"Changes?" she echoed, apprehension in her voice. "What sort of changes?"

"I need to look over the place before I make any concrete decisions, but the location is perfect for a resort." Absently, he brushed the dust off his finger on the windowsill and gazed out. "Pool, tennis courts, health club, a face lift for the building itself."

"There's nothing wrong with this building. We don't cater to the resort set, Mr. Reynolds." Furious, B.J. approached the desk again. "This is an inn, with all the connotations that includes. Family-style meals, comfortable lodgings and a quiet atmosphere. That's why our guests come back."

"The clientele would increase with a few modern attractions," he countered coolly. "Particularly with the proximity to Lake Champlain."

"Keep your hot tubs and disco lounges for your other acquisitions." B.J. bypassed simmer and went straight to boil. "This is Lakeside, Vermont, not L.A. I don't want any plastic surgery on my inn."

Brows rose, and his mouth curved in a grim smile. "Your inn, Miss Clark?"

"That's right," she retorted, "You may hold the purse strings, Mr. Reynolds, but I know this place, and our guests come back year after year because of what we represent. There's no way you're going to change one brick."

"Miss Clark." Taylor stood menacingly over her. "If I choose to tear down this inn brick by brick, that's precisely what I'll do. Whatever alterations I make or don't make, remain my decision, and my decision alone. Your position as manager does not entitle you to a vote."

"And your position as owner doesn't entitle you to brains!" she was unable to choke back as she stomped from the office in a flurry of flying braids.

Chapter Two

With relish, B.J. slammed the door to her room. Arrogant, interfering, insufferable man. Why doesn't he go play Monopoly somewhere else? Doesn't he already have enough hotels to tinker with? There must be a hundred in the Reynolds chain in the states alone, plus all those elegant foreign resorts. Why doesn't he open one in Antarctica?

Abruptly, she caught sight of her reflection in the mirror and stared in disbelief. Her face was smudged. Dust clung to her sweatshirt and jeans. Her braids hung to her shoulders. All in all, she thought grimly, I look like a rather dim-witted ten-year-old. She suddenly noticed a line down her cheek, and lifting her hand, recalled Taylor's finger resting there.

"Oh, blast." Shaking her head, she began to quickly unbind her hair. "I made a mess of it," she muttered and stripped off her morning uniform. "Looking like a grimy teenager and then losing my temper on top of it. Well, he's not going to fire me," she vowed fiercely and stalked to the shower. "I'll quit first! I'm not staying around and watching my inn mutilated."

Thirty minutes later, B.J. pulled a brush through her hair and studied the new reflection with satisfaction. Soft clouds of wheat floated on her shoulders. She wore an ivory dress, nipped at the waist, belted in scarlet to match tiny blazing rubies at her ears. Heels gave her height a slight advantage. She felt confident she could no longer be mistaken for sixteen. Lifting a neatly written page from her dresser, she moved purposefully from the room, prepared to confront the bear in his den.

After a brief excuse for a knock, B.J. pushed open the office door and slowly and purposefully advanced towards the man sitting behind the desk. Shoving the paper under his nose, she waited for his brown eyes to meet hers.

"Ah, B.J. Clark, I presume. This is quite a transfiguration." Leaning back in his chair, Taylor allowed his eyes to travel over the length of her. "Amazing," he smiled into her resentful grey eyes, "what can be concealed under a sweatshirt and baggy pants. . . . What's this?" He waved the paper idly, his eyes still appraising her.

"My resignation." Placing her palms on the desk, she leaned forward and prepared to give vent to her emotions. "And now that I am no longer in your employ, Mr. Reynolds, it'll give me

a great deal of pleasure to tell you what I think.
You are," she began as his brow rose at her tone,
"a dictatorial, capitalistic opportunist. You've
bought an inn which has for generations maintained its reputation for quality and personal
service, and in order to make a few more annual
dollars, you plan to turn it into a live-in amusement park. In doing so, you will not only have to
let the current staff go, some of whom have
worked here for twenty years, but you'll succeed
in destroying the integrity of the entire district.
This is not your average tourist town, it's a quiet,
settled community. People come here for fresh
air and quiet, not for a brisk tennis match or to
sweat in a sauna, and—"

"Are you finished, Miss Clark?" Taylor questioned. Instinctively she recognized the danger
in his lowered tones.

"No." Mustering her last resources of courage,
she set her shoulders and sent him a lethal
glare. "Go soak in your Jacuzzi!"

On her heel, she spun around and made for the
door only to find her back pressed into it as she
was whirled back into the room.

"Miss Clark," Taylor began, effectively holding
her prisoner by leaning over her, arms at either
side of her head. "I permitted you to clear your
system for two reasons. First, you're quite a
fabulous sight when your temper's in full gear. I
noticed that even when I took you for a rude
teenager. A lot of it has to do with your eyes
going from mist to smoke, it's very impressive.
That, of course," he added as she stared up at
him, unable to form a sound, "is strictly on a

personal level. Now on a professional plane, I am receptive to your opinions, if not to your delivery."

Abruptly, the door swung open, dislodging B.J. and tumbling her into a hard chest. "We found Julius's lunch," Eddie announced cheerfully and disappeared.

"You have a very enthusiastic staff," Taylor commented dryly as his arms propped her up against him. "Who the devil is Julius?"

"He's Mrs. Frank's Great Dane. She doesn't . . . she won't go anywhere without him."

"Does he have his own room?" His tone was gently mocking.

"No, he has a small run in the back."

Taylor smiled suddenly, his face close to hers. Power shot through her system like a bolt of electricity down a lightning rod. With a jerk, she pulled away and pushed at her tumbled hair.

"Mr. Reynolds," she began, attempting to retrieve her all too elusive dignity. He claimed her hand and pulled her back toward the desk, then pushed her firmly down on the chair.

"Do be quiet, Miss Clark" he told her in easy tones, settling behind the desk. "It's my turn now." She stared with a melding of astonishment and indignation.

"What I ultimately do with this inn is my decision. However, I will consider your opinion as you are intimate with this establishment and with the area and I, as yet, am not." Lifting B.J.'s resignation, Taylor tore it in half and dropped the pieces on the desk.

"You can't do that," she sputtered.

"I have just done it." The mild tone vibrated with authority.

B.J.'s eyes narrowed. "I can easily write another."

"Don't waste your paper," he advised, leaning back in his chair. "I have no intention of accepting your resignation at the moment. Later, I'll let you know. However," he added slowly, shrugging, "if you insist, I shall be forced to close down the inn for the next few months until I've found someone to replace you."

"It couldn't possibly take months to replace me," B.J. protested, but he was looking up at the ceiling as though lost in thought.

"Six months perhaps."

"Six months?" she frowned. "But you can't. We have reservations, it's nearly the summer season. All those people can't be disappointed. And the staff—the staff would be out of work."

"Yes." With an agreeable smile, he nodded and folded his hands on the desk.

Her eyes widened. "But—that's blackmail!"

"I think that term is quite correct." His amusement increased. "You catch on very quickly, Miss Clark."

"You can't be serious. You," she sputtered. "You wouldn't actually close the inn just because I quit."

"You don't know me well enough to be sure, do you?" His eyes were unfathomable and steady. "Do you want to chance it?"

Silence hung for a long moment, each measuring the other. "No," B.J. finally murmured, then repeated with more strength, "No, blast it, I can't! You know that already. But I certainly don't understand why."

"You don't have to know why," he interrupted with an imperious gesture of his hand.

Sighing, B.J. struggled not to permit temper to rule her tongue again. "Mr. Reynolds," she began in what she hoped was a reasonable tone, "I don't know why you find it so important for me to remain as manager of the inn, but—"

"How old are you, Miss Clark?" He cut her off again. She stared in perplexed annoyance.

"I hardly see . . ."

"Twenty, twenty-one?"

"Twenty-four," B.J. corrected, inexplicably compelled to defend herself. "But I don't see what that has to do with anything."

"Twenty-four," he repeated, obviously concluding she had finished one sentence and that was sufficient. "Chronologically, I have eight years on you, and professionally quite a bit more. I opened my first hotel when you were still leading cheers at Lakeside High."

"I never led cheers at Lakeside High," she said coldly.

"Be that as it may"—he gently inclined his head—"the arithmetic remains the same. My reason for wanting you to remain in your current position at the inn is quite simple. You know the staff, the clientele, the suppliers and so forth . . . during this transition period I need your particular expertise."

"All right, Mr. Reynolds." B.J. relaxed slightly, feeling the conversation had leveled off to a more professional plane. "But you should be aware, I will give you absolutely no cooperation in changing any aspect which I feel affects the inn's personality. In point of fact, I will do my best to be uncooperative."

"I'm sure you're quite skillful at that," Taylor said easily. B.J. was unsure whether the smile in his eyes was real or in her imagination. "Now that we understand each other, Miss Clark, I'd like to see the place and get an idea of how you run things. I should be fairly well briefed in two weeks."

"You can't possibly understand all I've been trying to tell you in that amount of time."

"I make up my mind quickly," he told her. Smiling, he studied her face. "When something's mine, I know what to do with it." His smile widened at her frown, and he rose. "If you want the inn to remain as is, you'd best stick around and make your sales pitch." Taking her arm, he hauled her up from the chair. "Let's take a look around."

With all the warmth of a January sky, B.J. took Taylor on a tour of the first floor, describing storage closets in minute detail. Throughout, he kept a hand firmly on her arm as if to remind her of his authority. The continued contact made her vaguely uneasy. His scent was musky and essentially male and he moved with a casualness which she felt was deceptive. His voice rolled deep and smooth, and several times, she found herself listening more to its cadence than to his words. Annoyed, she added to the layers of frost coating her tone.

It would be easier, she decided, if he were short and balding with a generous middle, or, perhaps, if he had a sturdy mole on his left cheek and a pair of chins. It's absolutely unfair for a man to look the way he does and have to fight him, she thought resentfully.

"Have I lost you, Miss Clark?"

"What?" Looking up, she collected her wits, inwardly cursing him again for possessing such dark, magnetic eyes. "No, I was thinking perhaps you'd like lunch." A very good improvisation, she congratulated herself.

"Fine." Agreeably, he allowed her to lead the way to the dining room.

It was a basic, rustic room, large and rectangular with beamed ceilings and gently faded wallpaper. Its charm was old and lasting; amber globed lamps, graceful antiques and old silver. Local stone dominated one wall in which a fireplace was set. Brass andirons guarded the empty hearth. Tables had been set to encourage sociability, with a few more secluded for intimate interludes. The air was humming with easy conversation and clattering dishes. A smell of fresh bread baking drifted toward them. In silence, Taylor studied the room, his eyes roaming from corner to corner until B.J. was certain he had figured the precise square footage.

"Very nice," he said simply.

A large, round man approached, lifting his head with a subtle dramatic flourish.

" 'If music be the food of love, play on.' "

" 'Give me excess of it, that, surfeiting the appetite may sicken, and so die.' "

Chuckling at B.J.'s response, he rolled with a regal, if oversized, grace into the dining room.

"Shakespeare at lunch?" Taylor inquired. B.J.

laughed; against her will her antagonism dissolved. "That was Mr. Leander. He's been coming to the inn twice a year for the past ten years. He used to tour with a low budget Shakespearean troupe, and he likes to toss lines at me for me to cap."

"And do you always have the correct response?"

"Luckily, I've always been fond of Shakespeare, and as insurance, I cram a bit when he makes his reservation."

"Just part of the service?" Taylor inquired, tilting his head to study her from a new angle.

"You could say that."

Prudently, B.J. scanned the room to see where the young Dobson twins were seated, then steered Taylor to a table as far distant as possible.

"B.J." Dot sidled to her side, eyes lighting on Taylor in pure feminine avarice. "Wilbur brought the eggs, and they're small again. Elsie's threatening to do permanent damage."

"All right, I'll take care of it." Ignoring Taylor's questioning stare, she turned to her waitress. "Dot, see to Mr. Reynolds' lunch. Please excuse me, Mr. Reynolds, I'll have to tend to this. Just send for me if you have any questions or if something is not to your satisfaction. Enjoy your meal."

Seeing Wilbur's eggs as a lucky escape hatch, B.J. hurried to the kitchen.

"Wilbur," she said with wicked enjoyment as the door swung shut behind her. "This time, I'm umpire."

A myriad of small demands dominated B.J.'s

afternoon. The art of diplomacy as well as the ability to delegate and make decisions was an intricate part of her job, and B.J. had honed her skills. She moved without breaking rhythm from a debate with the Dobson twins on the advisability of keeping a frog in their bathtub to a counseling service with one of the maids who was weeping into the fresh linen supply over the loss of a boyfriend. Through the hours of soothing and listening and laying down verdicts, she was still conscious of the presence of Taylor Reynolds. It was a simple matter to avoid him physically, but his presence seemed to follow her everywhere. He had made himself known, and she could not forget about him. Perversely, she found herself fretting to know where he was and what he was doing. Probably, she thought with a fresh flash of resentment, probably he's even now in my office poring over my books with a microscope, deciding where to put in his silly tennis courts or how to concrete the grove.

The dinner hour came and went. B.J. had decided to forego supervising the dining room to have a few hours of peace. When she came downstairs to the lounge the lighting was muted, the hour late. The three piece band hired for the benefit of the Saturday night crowd had already packed their equipment. The music had been replaced by the murmurs and clinking glasses of the handful of people who remained. It was the quiet time of the evening, just before silence. B.J. allowed her thoughts to drift back to Taylor.

I've got two weeks to make him see reason,

she reminded herself, exchanging goodnights as stragglers began to wander from the lounge. That should be plenty of time to make even the most insensitive businessman understand. I simply went about things in the wrong way. Tomorrow, I'll start my campaign with a brand new strategy. I'll keep my temper under control and use a great many smiles. I'm good at smiling when I put my mind to it.

Practicing her talent on the middle-aged occupant in room 224, B.J.'s confidence grew at his rapidly blinking appreciation. Yes, she concluded, smiles are much better than claws at this stage. A few smiles, a more sophisticated appearance, and a brisk, businesslike approach, and I'll defeat the enemy before the war's declared. Rejuvenated, she turned to the bartender who was lackadaisically wiping the counter. "Go on home, Don, I'll clear up the rest."

"Thanks, B.J." Needing no second urging, he dropped his rag and disappeared through the door.

"It's no trouble at all," she told the empty space with a magnanimous gesture of one hand. "I really insist."

Crossing the room, she began to gather half filled baskets of peanuts and empty glasses, switching on the small eye-level television for company. Around her, the inn settled for sleep, the groans and creaks so familiar, they went unnoticed. Now that the day was over, B.J. found the solitude for which she yearned.

Low, eerie music poured out of the television, drifting and floating through the darkened room. Glancing up, B.J. was soon mesmerized by a horror film. Kicking off her shoes, she slid onto a stool. The story was old and well-worn, but she was caught by a shot of clouds drifting over a full moon. She reached one hand absently for a basket of peanuts, settling them into her lap as the fog began to clear on the set to reveal the unknown terror, preceded by the rustle of leaves, and heavy breathing. With a small moan at the stalking monster's distorted face, B.J. covered her eyes and waited for doom to claim the heroine.

"You'd see more without your hand in front of your eyes."

As the voice came, disembodied in the darkness, B.J. shrieked, dislodging a shower of peanuts from her lap. "Don't ever do that again!" she commanded, glaring up at Taylor's grinning face.

"Sorry." The apology lacked conviction. Leaning on the bar, he nodded towards the set. "Why do you have it on if you don't want to watch?"

"I can't help myself, it's an obsession. But I always watch with my eyes closed. Now look, watch this part, I've seen it before." She grabbed his sleeve with one hand and pointed with the other. "She's going to walk right outside like an idiot. I ask you, would anyone with a working brain cell walk out into the pitch darkness when they hear something scraping at the window? Of course not," she answered for him. "A smart person would be huddled under the bed waiting for it to go away. Oh." She pulled him closer, burying her face against his chest as the monster's face loomed in a close-up. "It's horrible, I can't watch. Tell me when it's over."

Slowly, it dawned on her that she was burrowing into his chest, his heartbeat steady against her ear. His fingers tangled in her hair, smoothing and soothing her as though comforting a child. She stiffened and started to pull back, but the hand in her hair kept her still.

"No, wait a minute, he's still stalking about and leering. There." He patted her shoulder and loosened his grip. "Saved by commercial television."

Set free, B.J. fumbled off the stool and began gathering scattered peanuts and composure. "I'm afraid things got rather out of hand this afternoon, Mr. Reynolds." Her voice was not quite steady, but she hoped he would attribute the waver to cowardice. "I must apologize for not completing your tour of the inn."

He watched as she scrambled over the floor on her hands and knees, a curtain of pale hair concealing her face. "That's all right. I wandered a bit on my own. I finally met Eddie when not in motion. He's a very intense young man."

She shifted away from him to search for more far reaching nuts. "He'll be good at hotel management in a couple years. He just needs a little more experience." Keeping her face averted, B.J. waited for the heat to cool from her cheeks.

"I met quite a few of the inn's guests today. Everyone seems very fond of B.J." He closed the distance between them and pushed back the hair which lay across her cheek. "Tell me, what does it stand for?"

"What?" Diverted by the fingers on her skin, she found it hard to concentrate on the conversation.

35

"B.J." He smiled into bemused eyes. "What does it stand for?"

"Oh." She returned the smile, stepping strategically out of reach. "I'm afraid that's a closely guarded secret. I've never even told my mother."

Behind her, the heroine gave a high-pitched, lilting scream. Scattering nuts again, B.J. threw herself into Taylor's arms.

"Oh, I'm sorry, that caught me off guard." Mortified, she lifted her face and attempted to pull away.

"No, this is the third time in one day you've been in this position." One hand lifted, and traveled down the length of her hair as he held her still. "This time, I'm going to see what you taste like."

Before she could protest, his mouth lowered to hers, at once firm and possessing. His arm around her waist brought her close to mold against him. His tongue found hers, and she was unaware whether he had parted her lips or if they had done so of their own volition. He lingered over her mouth, savoring its softness, deepening the kiss until she clung to him for balance. She told herself the sudden spiraling of her heartbeat was a reaction to the horror movie, the quick dizziness, the result of a missed dinner. Then she told herself nothing and only experienced.

"Very nice." Taylor's murmured approval trailed along her cheekbone, moving back to tease the corner of her mouth. "Why don't we try it again?"

In instinctive defense, she pressed her hand

into his chest to ward him off. *Lightly*, she told herself, praying for the earth to stop trembling, *treat it lightly*. "I'm afraid I don't come in thirty-two flavors, Mr. Reynolds, and . . ."

"Taylor," he interrupted, smiling down at the hand which represented no more of an obstacle than a blade of grass. "I decided this morning, when you stalked me in the office, that we're going to know each other very well."

"Mr. Reynolds . . ."

"Taylor," he repeated, his eyes close and compelling. "And my decisions are always final."

"Taylor," she agreed, not wanting to debate a minor point when the distance between them was lessening despite the pressure against his chest. "Do you engage in this sort of activity with all the managers of your hotels?" Hoping to wound him with a scathing remark, B.J. was immediately disappointed when he tossed back his head and laughed.

"B.J., this current activity has nothing whatever to do with your position at the inn. I am merely indulging my weakness for women who look good in pigtails."

"Don't you kiss me again!" she ordered, struggling with a sudden desperation which surprised him into loosening his hold.

"You'll have to choose between being demure or being provocative, B.J." His tone was mild, but she saw as she backed away, his eyes had darkened with temper. "Either way we play, I'm going to win, but it would make the game easier to follow."

"I don't play this sort of game," she retorted, "and I am neither demure nor provocative."

"You're a bit of both." His hands slipped into his pockets, and he rocked gently on his heels as he studied her furious face. "It's an intriguing combination." His brow lifted in speculation. An expression of amusement flitted over his features. "But I suppose you already know that or you wouldn't be so good at it."

Forgetting her fears, B.J. took a step towards him. "The only thing I know is that I have absolutely no desire to intrigue you in any way. All that I want you to do is to keep your resort builder's hands off this inn." Her hands balled into tight fists. "I wish you'd go back to New York and sit in your penthouse."

Before he could answer, B.J. turned and darted from the room. She hurried through the darkened lobby without even a backward glance.

Chapter Three

B.J. decided that making a fool of herself the previous evening had been entirely Taylor Reynolds' responsibility. Today, she resolved, slipping a gray blazer over a white silk shirt, *I will be astringently businesslike.* Nonetheless, she winced at the memory of her naive plea that he not kiss her again, the absurd way her voice had shaken with the words. *Why didn't I come up with some cool, sophisticated retort?* she asked herself. *Because I was too busy throwing peanuts around the room and making a fool of myself,* she answered the question to her frowning mirror image. *Why did a simple kiss cloak my brain with layers of cheesecloth?* The woman in the mirror stared back without answering.

He had caught her off guard, B.J. decided as she arranged her hair in a neat, businesslike roll at her neck's nape. It was so unexpected, she had overreacted. Despite herself, she relived the sensation of his mouth claiming hers, his breath warm on her cheek. The knee trembling, brain spinning feeling never before experienced, washed over her again, and briskly, she shook her head to dispel it. It was simply a matter of the unexpected creating a false intenseness, like pricking your thumb with a needle while sewing.

It was important, she knew, to refrain from thinking of Taylor Reynolds on a personal level, and to remember he held the fate of the Lakeside Inn in his hands.

Dirty pool, her mind muttered, recalling his easy threat to close the inn if she pressed her resignation. Emotional blackmail. He knew he held all the aces, and waited, with that damnably appealing smile, for her to fold or call. *Well*, she decided, and smoothed the charcoal material of her skirt, *I play a pretty mean game of poker myself, Taylor Reynolds*. After trying out several types of smiles in the mirror, polite, condescending, dispassionate, she left the room with brisk steps.

Sunday mornings were usually quiet. Most of the guests slept late, rising in dribbles to wander downstairs for breakfast. Traditionally, B.J. spent these quiet hours closeted in her office with whatever paperwork she felt merited attention. From experience, she had found this particular system worked well, being the least likely time for calamities, minor or major, to befall guests or staff.

She grabbed a quick coffee in the kitchen before plunging into the sea of invoices and account books.

"How providential." She jerked slightly as a hand captured her arm, and she found herself being led to the dining room. "Now, I won't have to have breakfast alone."

The dozens of flaming retorts which sprang to mind at Taylor's presumptuousness were dutifully banked down. B.J. answered with her seasoned polite smile. "How kind of you to ask. I hope you spent a pleasant night."

"As stated in your public relations campaign, the inn is conducive to restful nights."

Waving aside her hostess, B.J. moved through the empty tables to a corner booth. "I think you'll find all my publicity is based on fact, Mr. Reynolds." Sliding in, B.J. struggled to keep her voice light and marginally friendly. Remnants of their argument in her office and their more personal encounter in the lounge clung to her, and she attempted to erase both from her mind.

"So far I find no discrepancies."

Maggie hovered by the table, her smile dreamily absent. No doubt she was thinking of her date last night with Wally, B.J. thought. "Toast and coffee, Maggie," she said kindly, breaking the trance. The waitress scribbled on her pad, her cheeks flushed.

"You know," Taylor observed after giving his order, "you're very good at your job."

B.J. chided herself for her pleasure at the unexpected praise. "Why do you say that?"

"Not only are your books in perfect order, but

41

you know your staff and handle them with unobtrusive deftness. You just managed to convey a five minute lecture with one brief look."

"It makes it easier when you understand your staff and their habits." Her brows lifted in easy humor. "You see, I happen to know Maggie's mind is still focused on the double feature she and Wally didn't watch last night."

His grin flashed, boyish and quick.

"The staff is very much like a family." B.J. was careful to keep her tone casual, her hands busy pouring coffee. "The guests feel that. They enjoy the informality which is always accompanied by quality service. Our rules are flexible, and the staff is trained to adjust to the individual needs of the guests. The inn is a basic place, not for those who require formal entertainment or unlimited luxury. Fresh air, good food and a pleasant atmosphere are our enticements, and we deliver."

She paused as Maggie placed their breakfast order on the table.

"Do you have a moral objection to resorts, B.J.?"

The unexpectedness of Taylor's question put her off. Blinking in confusion at the long, lean fingers as they held a knife, spreading Betty Jackson jelly on toast, she stammered, "No . . . why of course not." Those fingers, she recalled irrelevantly, had tangled in her hair. "No," she repeated more firmly, meeting his eyes. "Resorts are fine if they are run correctly, as yours are. But their function is entirely different from ours. In a proper resort there's an activity for every minute of the day. Here, the atmosphere is more relaxed, a little fishing or boating, skiing, and above all the menu. The Lakeside Inn is perfect exactly as it is," she concluded more fiercely than she had intended and watched one brow rise, nearly meeting the curling thickness of his hair.

"That's yet to be determined." He lifted his cup to his lips.

His tone was mild, but B.J. recognized traces of anger in the disconcertingly direct eyes. She dropped her eyes to her own cup as if enticed by the rich, black liquid.

"'The gray-eyed morn smiles on the frowning night.'"

The quote brought her head up sharply, and looking into Mr. Leander's smiling, expectant face, B.J. searched her brain. "'Chequering the eastern clouds with streaks of light.'"

Thank goodness I've read *Romeo and Juliet* a dozen times, she thought, watching his pleased saunter as he moved to his table.

"One day, he's going to catch you, and you're going to draw a blank."

"Life's a series of risks," she returned flippantly. "Better to accept its challenges."

Reaching over, he tucked a stray lock behind her ear, and she jerked away from his touch, unexpectedly shy.

"For the most part," he drew the words out with infuriating emphasis, "I believe you do. It should make things very interesting. More coffee?" His question was pleasant and easy as if they had shared the morning meal on a regular basis. B.J. shook her head in refusal. . . . She felt uneasily inept at parrying words with this domineering, sophisticated man. . . .

Sunlight poured through the many-paned windows, spilling in patchwork patterns on the floor, a lawn mower hummed along the outer edges of lawn, and somewhere close, a bird sang his enjoyment of a golden day. Closeted in the office with Taylor, B.J. tuned even these small pleasures out, keeping her mind firmly on the business at hand. Here, with the impersonal wedge of invoices and account books between them, she felt confident and assured. In discussing the inn's procedure, her feet were on solid ground. Honesty forced her to admit that Taylor Reynolds knew his profession down to the finest detail. He skimmed through her books with the sharp eye of an accountant, shifted and sorted invoices with the ease of a business manager.

At least, B.J. told herself, he doesn't treat me like an empty-headed imbecile who can't tally monthly accounts. Rather, she found him listening to her explanations with attentive respect. Soothed by his obvious appreciation of her intelligence B.J. decided if he did not yet look on the Lakeside Inn as she did, perhaps that too would come.

"I see you deal with a great many small businesses and local farms."

"That's right." She searched the bottom drawer of her desk for an ashtray as he lit a cigarette. "It's advantageous on all sides. We get more personal service and fresher produce, and it boosts local economy." Finding a small ceramic ashtray under a pile of personal correspondence, B.J. placed it on the desk. "The Lakeside Inn is essential to this district. We provide employment and a market for local products and services."

"Umm."

Finding his response less than illuminating, B.J. opened her mouth to continue when the door burst open.

"B.J." Eddie stood, bottom lip trembling. "It's the Bodwins."

"I'll be right there." Suppressing a sigh, she made a mental note to tell Eddie to knock during Taylor's stay.

"Is that a natural disaster or a plague?" Taylor asked, watching Eddie's speedy exit.

"It's nothing, really." She edged towards the door. "Excuse me, I'll just be a minute."

Shutting the door behind her, B.J. hurried to the lobby.

"Hello, Miss Patience, Miss Hope." She greeted the elderly Bodwin sisters with a wary smile.

Tall and lean as two aged willows, the Bodwins were long-standing guests.

"It's so nice to see you both again."

"It's always a pleasure to come back, Miss Clark," Miss Patience announced, and Miss Hope murmured in agreement. Habitually Miss Patience announced, and Miss Hope murmured. It was one of the few things which separated them. Over the years they had melded into mirror images from their identical wire rimmed spectacles to their identical orthopedic shoes.

"Eddie, see that the luggage is taken up,

please." Miss Patience flashed a knowing smile which B.J. tried not to notice. B.J. saw her sharp-eyed glance drift over her head. Turning, she spotted Taylor.

"Miss Patience, Miss Hope, this is Taylor Reynolds, the owner of the inn." Miss Patience shot her a meaningful look.

"A pleasure, ladies." Gallantly, he took each thin boned hand in his. A blush, dormant for twenty-five years, rose to Miss Hope's wrinkled cheek.

"You're a very fortunate young man." Miss Patience gave Taylor a thorough survey, then nodded as if satisfied. "I'm sure you know what a treasure you have in Miss Clark. I hope you appreciate her."

B.J. resisted grinding her teeth for fear the sound would be audible. With a smile, Taylor laid a hand on her shoulder.

"I'm quite convinced Miss Clark is indispensable and my appreciation inadequate."

Satisfied, Miss Patience nodded.

B.J. shook the offending hand from her shoulder and assumed a coolly professional manner. "You have your regular table, number 2."

"Of course." Miss Patience moved her lips into a smile and patted B.J.'s cheek. "You're a good girl, Miss Clark." Smiling vaguely, the two ladies drifted away.

"Surely, B.J." Taylor turned to B.J. with an infuriating smile, "you're not going to give those two dotty old girls the second table?"

"The Lakeside Inn," she said coldly, turning to precede him to the office, "makes it a habit to please its guests. I see no reason why the Bodwins shouldn't sit wherever they want. Mr. Campbell always seated them at Number 2."

"Mr. Campbell," Taylor countered with infuriating calm, "no longer owns the inn. I do."

"I'm well aware of that." Her chin tilted higher in defiance. "Do you want me to turn out the Bodwin sisters and place them at the table near the kitchen? Don't they look fancy enough for you? Why don't you think of them as people rather than little black numbers in the bloody account book?"

Her tirade was sharply cut off as he gripped her shoulders. She found she had swallowed the remaining words before she could prevent herself.

"You have," he began in an ominously low voice, "a very unfortunate temper and some very odd ideas. No one tells me how to run my business. Absolutely no one. Advice is accepted upon request, but I only make the decisions, and I alone give the orders."

He moved towards her. She could only stare, fascinated and faintly terrified.

"Do we understand each other?"

B.J. nodded, wide-eyed, then gathered courage to answer audibly. "Yes, perfectly. What would you like me to do about the Bodwins?"

"You've already done it. When you do something which displeases me, B.J., I'll let you know." The underlying threat brought storm warnings to her eyes. "Of course you know," Taylor continued, his tone softening, "you're a very ingenious lady. You've managed to share my breakfast table and work with me throughout the morning without once using my name.

You've skirted around it, jumped over it and crawled under it, fascinating me with the acrobatics."

"That's ridiculous." She attempted to shrug, but his hands were firm on her shoulders. "Your imagination needs re-oiling."

"Then perhaps . . ." His arms moved to capture her waist. She arched away only to be brought steadily closer. "You'd say it now." His mouth hovered above hers. She felt the unfamiliar sweet flow of weakness, the trembling warmth just under her skin.

"Taylor." She failed to bring her voice above a whisper.

"Very good, you'll use it more often." His mouth curved, but she saw the smile only in his eyes. "Do I frighten you, B.J.?"

"No." Her denial was faint. "No," she repeated with more firmness.

"Liar." His laugh was both amused and pleased as his mouth teased hers. It rubbed lightly, holding back the promise until with a moan she drew him closer and took it.

Her breasts crushed against his chest, her lips instinctively found his. She felt herself tumbling in helpless cartwheels down an endless shaft where lights whirled in speeding colors. His hands moved from her waist to her hips, his strong fingers discovering the secrets of subtle curves as his mouth took everything she offered. Craving more, she strained against him until her sharpened senses began to dim, and the world spun hazily around her and vanished.

Fear rose like a phoenix from the flames of passion, and she struggled away, stunned and confused. "I . . . I need to check how lunch is going." She fumbled behind for the doorknob.

His hands in his pockets, Taylor rocked back on his heels and held her gaze with steady assurance. "Of course. . . . Now run away to your duties. But you understand, B.J., that I intend to have you sooner or later. I can be patient up to a point."

Her hand connected with the knob. She found her voice. "Of all the appalling nerve! I'm not a piece of property you can have your agent pick up for you."

"No, I'm handling this strictly on my own." He smiled at her. "I know when something's going to be mine. Acquiring it is simply a matter of timing."

"I'm not an *it*." More outraged than she had thought possible, she took a step toward him. "I have no intention of being acquired and added to your trophies. And timing will get you no-where!"

His smile was maddeningly confident. B.J. slammed the door full force behind her.

Chapter Four

Mondays always kept B.J. busy. She was convinced that if a major calamity were to fall, it would fall on a Monday simply because that would be the time she would be least able to cope with it. Taylor Reynolds' presence in her office was an additional Monday morning burden. His calm statement of the previous day was still fresh in her mind, and she was still seething with resentment. In an icy voice, she explained to him each phone call she made, each letter she wrote, each invoice she filed. He would not, she decided, accuse her of being uncooperative. Frigid perhaps, she thought with wicked pleasure, but not uncooperative.

Taylor's impeccable, businesslike attitude did nothing to endear him to her. She was well aware that her cold politeness bordered on the insulting.

Never had she met a man more in control or more annoying. Briefly, she considered pouring her coffee into his lap just to get a reaction. The thought was satisfying.

"Did I miss a joke?" Taylor asked as an involuntary smile flitted over B.J.'s face.

"What?" Realizing her lapse, B.J. struggled to compose her features. "No, I'm afraid my mind was wandering. You'll have to excuse me," she went on, "I have to make sure that all the rooms are made up by this time of day. Will you be wanting lunch in here or in the dining room?"

"I'll come to the dining room." Leaning back, Taylor studied her as he tapped his pencil against the corner of the desk. "Are you joining me?"

"Oh, I'm terribly sorry." B.J.'s tone was falsely saccharine. "I'm swamped today. I recommend the roast beef, though. I'm sure you'll find it satisfactory." Satisfied with her delivery, she closed the door quietly behind her.

With ingenuity and luck, B.J. managed to avoid Taylor throughout the afternoon. The inn was nearly empty as most of the guests were outdoors enjoying the mild spring weather. B.J. was able to slip down the quiet corridors without running into Taylor. She kept her antenna tuned for his presence, however. Though she knew it was childish, she found herself enjoying the one-way game of hide and seek. It became a self-imposed challenge that she keep out of his sight until nightfall.

In the pre-dinner lull, the inn was drowsy and silent. Humming to herself, B.J. carefully checked off linens in the third floor supply room. She was confident Taylor would not venture into that area of the inn, and relaxed her guard. Her mind traveled from her task, touching on pictures of boating on the lake, walks in the woods, and long summer evenings. Though her daydreams were pleasant, they were underlined by a nagging dissatisfaction. She tried to shrug it off but found it stubborn. There was something missing from the images, or rather someone. Whom would she be boating with on the lake? Whom would she be walking with in the woods? Who would be there to make the long summer evenings special? A distressing image began to form in B.J.'s brain, and she squeezed her eyes tight until it faded.

"I don't need him," she muttered, giving a pile of freshly laundered sheets a pat. "Absolutely not." B.J. backed from the tiny room and quietly pulled the door shut. When she backed into a solid object, she shrieked and fell forward against the closed door.

"Jumpy, aren't you?" Taylor took her shoulders and turned her to face him. His expression was amused. "Muttering to yourself, too. Maybe you need a vacation."

"I . . . I . . ."

"A long vacation," he concluded, giving her cheek a fatherly pat.

Finding her tongue, B.J. responded with reasonable calm. "You startled me, sneaking around that way."

"I thought it was a rule of the house," he countered as his grin broke out. "You've been doing it all afternoon."

Furious that her cunning had fallen short of the mark, she spoke with frosty dignity. "I have no idea what you're talking about. Now, if you'll excuse me . . ."

"Did you know you get a half-inch vertical line between your eyebrows when you're annoyed?"

"I'm very busy." She kept her voice cool as she did her best to keep the space between her brows smooth. *Blast the man!* she thought as his engaging smile began to have its effect on her. "Taylor, if there is something specific you want . . ." She stopped as she saw his grin widen until it nearly split his face. "If there's some business you want to discuss—" she amended.

"I took a message for you," he informed her, then lifted a finger to smooth away the crease between her brows. "A very intriguing message."

"Oh?" she said casually, wishing he would back up so that she did not feel so imprisoned between his body and the closed store-room door.

"Yes, I wrote it down so there'd be no mistake." He took a slip of paper from his pocket and read. "It's from a Miss Peabody. She wanted you to know that Cassandra had her babies. Four girls and two boys. Sextuplets." Taylor lowered the paper and shook his head. "Quite an amazing feat."

"Not if you're a cat." B.J. felt the color lacing her cheeks. *Why would he have to be the one to take the message? Why couldn't Cassandra have waited?* "Miss Peabody is one of our oldest guests. She stays here twice a year."

"I see," said Taylor, his mouth twitching. "Well, now that I've done my duty, it's your turn to do yours." Taking her hand, Taylor began to lead her down the corridor. "This country air gives me quite an appetite. You know the menu, what do you recommend we have?"

"I can't possibly," she began.

"Of course you can," he interrupted mildly. "Just think of me as a guest. Inn policy is to give the guests what pleases them. It pleases me to have dinner with you."

Cornered by her own words, B.J. offered no argument. Within minutes, she found herself seated across from the man she had so successfully avoided during the afternoon.

B.J. thought dinner a relatively painless affair. She felt too, as it neared an end, that she had done her duty and done it superbly. It was, however, difficult to resist the pull of Taylor's charm when he chose to put it into use. The charm itself was so natural and understated that she often found herself captivated before she realized what was happening. Whenever she felt her walls of indifference crumbling, she retreated a step and shored up the holes. *What a shame he isn't someone else*, she mused as he recounted an anecdote. *It would be so nice to enjoy a quiet dinner with him if there weren't any boundaries. But there are*, she reminded herself, quickly pulling out of the range of his charm. *Very definite, very important boundaries. This is war*, she reflected, thinking of their conversation of the previous day. *I can't afford to get caught behind enemy lines*. As Taylor raised his glass and smiled at her, B.J.

wondered if Mata Hari had ever been faced with a tougher assignment.

They had reached the coffee stage when Eddie approached their table. "Mr. Reynolds?" B.J. looked on with approval as Eddie neither fidgeted nor seemed ready to burst with the tidings he bore. "There's a phone call for you from New York."

"Thank you, Eddie. I'll take it in the office. I shouldn't be long," Taylor told her as he rose.

"Please, don't rush on my account." B.J. gave him a careful smile, resigning herself to the fact she was a coward. "I still have several things to see to this evening."

"I'll see you later," Taylor returned in a tone that brooked no argument. Their eyes met in a quick clash of wills. In a swift change of mood, Taylor laughed and bent down to kiss B.J. on the forehead before he strolled away.

Mouth agape, B.J. rubbed the spot with her fingertips, wondering why she suddenly felt lightheaded. Forcing herself back to earth, she drank her coffee and hurried off to the lounge.

Monday nights at the inn were an old tradition. The lounge was the center of activity for the weekly event. As B.J. paused in the doorway, she ran a critical eye over the room. The candles had been lit inside each of the coach lanterns which sat on the huddled tables. The lights flickered against the wood. Scents of polish, old wood and smoke melded. The dance floor was gently lit with amber spotlights. Satisfied that the mood was set, B.J. crossed the room and halted next to an ancient Victrola. The faithful mechanism was housed in a rich mahogany cabinet. With affection, B.J. trailed a finger over the smooth lid before opening it.

People began to wander in as she sorted through the collection of old 78s. The hum of conversation behind her was so familiar, it barely tickled her consciousness. Glasses chinked, ice rattled, and an occasional laugh echoed along the walls. With the absentminded skill of an expert, B.J. wound the Victrola into life and set a thick, black record on the turntable. The music which drifted out was scratchy, tinny and charming. Before the record was half over, three couples were on the dance floor. Another Monday night was launched.

During the next half hour, B.J. played an unbroken stream of nineteen-thirty tunes. Over the years, she had noted that no matter what the mean age of the audience, the response to a trip through the past was positive. *Perhaps,* she mused, *it's because the simplicity of the music suits the simplicity of the inn.* With a shrug, she abandoned her analysis and grinned at a couple fox-trotting over the dance floor to the strains of "Tea For Two."

"What the devil is going on in here?"

B.J. heard the demanding question close to her ear and whirled to find herself face to face with Taylor. "Oh, I see you're finished with your call. I hope there isn't any trouble?"

"Nothing important." He waited until she had switched records before he asked again, "B.J., I asked you what's going on in here."

"Why, just what it looks like," she answered vaguely, hearing from the tone of the record that it was time to replace the needle. "Sit down,

Taylor, I'll have Don mix you a drink. You know, I'd swear there hasn't been time for this needle to wear out." Delving into her spares, B.J. began the task of changing needles.

"When you're finished, perhaps you'd take a look at my carburetor."

Engrossed in the intricacies of her job, B.J. remained untouched by Taylor's mockery. "We'll see," she murmured, then carefully placed the new needle on the record. "What would you like, Taylor?" As she straightened, she glanced towards the bar.

"Initially, an explanation."

"An explanation?" she repeated, finally giving him her full attention. "An explanation about what?"

"B.J." Impatience was beginning to thread through his tone. "Are you being deliberately dense?"

Liking neither his tone nor his question, B.J. stiffened. "Perhaps if you would be a bit more specific, I would be a bit less dense."

"I was under the impression that this lounge possessed a functional P.A. system."

"Well, of course it does." As she became more confused, B.J. pushed away the thought that perhaps she actually was dense. "What does that have to do with anything?"

"Why isn't it being used?" He glanced down at the Victrola. "And why are you using this archaic piece of equipment?"

"The P.A. system isn't being used," she explained in calm, reasonable tones, "because it's Monday."

"I see." Taylor glanced toward the dance floor

where one couple was instructing another on the proper moves of a two step. "That, of course, explains everything."

His sarcasm caused indignation to flood through her. Clamping her teeth on a stream of unwise remarks, B.J. began to sift rapidly through records. "On Monday nights, we use the Victrola and play old records. And it is not an archaic piece of equipment," she added, unable to prevent herself. "It's an antique, a museum quality antique."

"B.J." Taylor spoke to the top of her head as she bent to change records. "Why?"

"Why what?" she snapped, furious with his ambiguity.

"Why do you use the Victrola and play old records on Monday nights?" He spoke very clearly, spacing his words as if speaking to someone whose brain was not fully operative.

"Because," B.J. began, her eyes flowing, her fists clenching.

Taylor held up a hand to halt the ensuing explanation. "Wait." After the one word command, he crossed the room and spoke to one of the guests. Seething, B.J. watched him use his most charming smile. It faded as he moved back to join her. "You're being relieved of Victrola duty for a bit. Outside." With this, he took her arm and pulled her to the side door. The cool night air did nothing to lower B.J.'s temperature. "Now." Taylor closed the door behind him and leaned back against the side of the building. He made a small gesture with his hand. "Go right ahead."

"Oh, you make me so mad I could scream!"

With this dire threat, B.J. began pacing up and down the porch. "Why do you have to be so . . . so . . ."

"Officious?" Taylor offered.

"Yes!" B.J. agreed, wishing passionately that she had thought of the word herself. "Everything's moving along just fine, and then you have to come in and look down your superior nose." For some moments, she paced in silence. The romance of the moonlight filtering through the trees seemed sadly out of place. "People are enjoying themselves in there." She swung her hand towards the open window. A Cole Porter number drifted back to her. "You don't have any right to criticize it. Just because we're not using a live band, or playing top forty numbers, doesn't mean we're not entertaining the guests. I really don't see why you have to . . ." She broke off abruptly as he grabbed her arm.

"O.K., time's up." As he spun her around, the hair fell over B.J.'s face, and she brushed it back impatiently. "Now, suppose we start this from the beginning."

"You know," she said between her teeth, "I really hate it when you're calm and patient."

"Stick around," he invited. It began to sink into her brain that his voice was dangerously low. "You might see the other end of the scale." Glaring at him did not seem to improve her situation, but B.J. continued to do so. "If you'll think back to the beginning of this remarkable conversation, you'll recall that I asked you a very simple question. And, I believe, a very reasonable one."

"And I told you," she tossed out, then faltered.

"At least, I think I did." Frustrated, she threw both hands up in the air. "How am I supposed to remember what you said and what I said? It took you ten minutes to come to the point in the first place." She let out a deep breath as she realized she did not yet have control of her temper. "All right, what was your very simple, very reasonable question?"

"B.J., you would try the patience of a saint." She heard the amused exasperation in his voice and tried not to be charmed. "I would like to know why I stepped into nineteen-thirty-five when I came into the lounge."

"Every Monday night," she began in crisp, practical tones, "the inn offers this sort of entertainment. The Victrola was brought here more than fifty years ago, and it's been used every Monday night since. Guests who've been here before expect it. Of course," she went on, too involved in her story to realize she was being drawn closer into Taylor's arms, "the P.A. system was installed years ago. The other six nights of the week, we switch off between it and a live band, depending on the season. The Monday night gathering is almost as old as the inn itself and an important part of our tradition."

The low, bluesy notes of "Embraceable You" were floating through the open window. B.J. was swaying to its rhythm, as yet unaware that Taylor was leading her in a slow dance. "The guests look forward to it. I've found since I've worked here, that's true no matter how old or how young the clientele is." Her voice had lost its crispness. She found her trend of thought slipping away from her as their bodies swayed to the soft music.

"That was a very reasonable answer." Taylor drew her closer, and she tilted back her head, unwilling to break eye contact. "I'm beginning to see the advantages of the idea myself." Their faces were close, so close she could feel the touch of his breath on her lips. "Cold?" he asked, feeling her tremble. Though she shook her head, he gathered her closer until the warmth of his body crept into hers. Their cheeks brushed as they merged into one gently swaying form.

"I should go back in," she murmured, making no effort to move away. She closed her eyes and let his arms and the music guide her.

"Um-hum." His mouth was against her ear.

Small night sounds added to the lull of the music from the lounge; a whisper of leaves, the quiet call of a bird, the flutter of moth wings against window glass. The air was soft and cool on B.J.'s shoulders. It was touched with the light scent of hyacinth. Moonlight sprinkled through the maples, causing the shadows to tremble. She could feel Taylor's heartbeat, a sure, steady rhythm against her own breast. He trailed his mouth along her temple, brushing it through her hair as his hands roamed along her back.

B.J. felt her will dissolving as her senses grew more and more acute. She could hear the sound of his breathing over the music, feel the texture of his skin beneath his shirt, taste the male essence of him on her tongue. Her surroundings were fading like an old photograph with only Taylor remaining sharp and clear. Untapped desire swelled inside her. Suddenly, she felt herself being swallowed by emotions she was not prepared for, by needs she could not understand.

"No, please." Her bid for freedom was so swift and unexpected that she broke from Taylor's arms without a struggle. "I don't want this." She clung to the porch rail and faced him.

Closing the distance between them in one easy motion, Taylor circled the back of her neck with his hand. "Yes, you do." His mouth lowered, claiming hers. B.J. felt the porch tilt under her feet.

Longing, painfully sweet, spread through her until she felt she would suffocate. His hands were bringing her closer and closer. With some unexplained instinct, she knew if she were wrapped in his arms again, she would never find the strength to resist him.

"No!" Lifting both hands, she pushed against his chest and freed herself. "I don't!" she cried in passionate denial. Turning, she streaked down the porch steps. "Don't tell me what I want," she flung back at him before she raced around the side of the building.

She paused before she entered the inn to catch her breath and to allow her pounding heart to slow down. Certainly not the usual Monday evening at Lakeside Inn, she thought, smiling wryly to herself. Unconsciously, she hummed a few bars of "Embraceable You," but caught herself with a self-reprimanding frown before she entered the kitchen to remind Dot about the bud vases on the breakfast tables.

Chapter Five

There are days when nothing goes right. The morning, blue and clear and breezy, looked deceptively promising. Clad in a simple green shirtdress and low heels, B.J. marched down the stairs running the word *businesslike* over and over in her mind. Today, she determined, she would be the manager of the inn conducting business with the owner of the inn. There was no moonlight, no music, and she would not forget her responsibilities again. She strolled into the dining room, prepared to greet Taylor casually, then use the need to oversee breakfast preparations as an excuse not to share the morning meal with him. Taylor, however, was already well into a fluffy mound of scrambled eggs and deep into a conversation with Mr. Leander. Taylor gave B.J. an absent wave as she entered, then returned his full attention to his breakfast companion.

Perversely, B.J. was annoyed that her well-planned excuse was unnecessary. She scowled at the back of Taylor's head before she flounced into the kitchen. Ten minutes later, she was told in no uncertain terms that she was in the way. Banished to her office, she sulked in private.

For the next thirty minutes, B.J. occupied herself with busy work, all the while keeping her ears pricked for Taylor's approach. As the minutes passed, she felt a throbbing tension build at the base of her neck. The stronger the ache became, the deeper became her resentment towards Taylor. She set the reason for her headache and her glum mood at his doorstep, though she could not have answered what he had done to cause either. *He was here*, she decided, then broke the point of her pencil. *That was enough.*

"B.J.!" Eddie swirled into the office as she stood grinding her teeth and sharpening her pencil. "There's trouble."

"You bet there is," she muttered.

"It's the dishwasher." Eddie lowered his eyes as if announcing a death in the family. "It broke down in the middle of breakfast."

B.J. let out her breath in a quick sound of annoyance. "All right, I'll call Max. With any luck it'll be going full swing before lunch."

Luck, B.J. was to find, was a mirage.

An hour later, she stood by as Max the repairman did an exploratory on the dishwasher. She found his continual mutters, tongue cluckings and sighs wearing on her nerves. Time was fleeting, and it seemed to her that Max was working at an impossibly slow pace. Impatient, she leaned over his shoulder and stared at tubes and wires. Bracing one hand on Max's back, she leaned in further and pointed.

"Couldn't you just . . ."

"B.J." Max sighed and removed another screw. "Go play with the inn and let me do my job."

Straightening, B.J. stuck out her tongue at the back of his head, then flushed scarlet as she spotted Taylor standing inside the doorway.

"Have a problem?" he asked. Though his voice and mouth were sober, his eyes laughed at her. She found his silent mockery infuriating.

"I can handle it," she snapped, wishing her cheeks were cool and her position dignified. "I'm sure you must be very busy." She cursed herself for hinting at his morning involvement. This time he did smile, and she cursed him as well.

"I'm never too busy for you, B.J." Taylor crossed the room, then took her hand and raised it to his lips before she realized his intent. Max cleared his throat.

"Cut that out." She tore her hand away and whipped it behind her back. "There's no need to concern yourself with this," she continued, struggling to assume the businesslike attitude she had vowed to take. "Max is fixing the dishwasher before the lunch rush."

"No, I'm not." Max sat back on his heels and shook his head. In his hand was a small-toothed wheel.

"What do you mean, no you're not?" B.J. demanded, forgetting Taylor in her amazement. "You've got to. I need . . ."

"What you need is one of these," Max interrupted, holding up the wheel.

"Well, all right." B.J. plucked the part from his hand and scowled at it. "Put one in. I don't see how a silly little thing like this could cause all this trouble."

"When the silly little thing has a broken tooth, it can cause a lot of trouble," Max explained patiently, and glanced at Taylor for masculine understanding. "B.J., I don't carry things like this in stock. You'll have to get it from Burlington."

"Burlington?" Realizing the situation was desperate B.J. used her most pleading look. "Oh, but, Max."

Though well past his fiftieth birthday, Max was not immune to huge gray eyes. He shifted from one foot to the other, sighed and took the part from B.J.'s palm. "All right, all right, I'll drive into Burlington myself. I'll have the machine fixed before dinner, but lunch is out. I'm not a magician."

"Thank you, Max." Rising on her toes, B.J. pecked his cheek. "What would I do without you?" Mumbling, he packed up his tools and started out of the room. "Bring your wife in for dinner tonight, on the house." Pleased with her success, B.J. smiled as the door swung shut. When she remembered Taylor, she cleared her throat and turned to him.

"You should have those eyes registered with the police department," he advised, tilting his head and studying her. "They're a lethal weapon."

"I don't know what you're talking about." She

sniffed with pretended indifference while she wished she could have negotiated with Max in private.

"Of course you do." With a laugh, Taylor cupped her chin in his hand. "That look you aimed at him was beautifully timed."

"I'm sure you're mistaken, she replied, wishing his mere touch would not start her heart pounding. "I simply arranged things in the best interest of the inn. That's my job."

"So it is," he agreed, and leaned on the injured dishwasher. "Do you have any suggestions as to what's to be done until this is fixed?"

"Yes." She glanced at the double stainless steel sink. "Roll up your sleeves."

It did not occur to B.J. to be surprised that she and Taylor washed the dozens of breakfast dishes side by side until it was *fait accompli*. The interlude had been odd, B.J. felt, because of the unusual harmony which existed between them. They had enjoyed a companionable banter, an easy partnership without the tension which habitually entered their encounters. When Elsie returned to begin lunch preparations, they scarcely noticed her.

"Not one casualty," Taylor proclaimed as B.J. set the last plate on its shelf.

"That's only because I saved two of yours from crashing on the floor."

"Slander," Taylor stated and swung an arm over her shoulder as he led her from the room. "You'd better be nice to me. What'll you do if Max doesn't fix the dishwasher before dinner? Think of all those lunch dishes."

"I'd rather not. However, I've already given

that possibility some consideration." B.J. found the handiest chair in her office and dropped into it. "I know a couple of kids in town that we could recruit in a pinch. But Max won't let me down."

"You have a lot of faith." Taylor sat behind the desk, then lifted his feet to rest on top of it.

"You don't know Max," B.J. countered. "If he said he'd have it fixed before dinner, he will. Otherwise, he'd have said I'll try, or maybe I can, or something of that sort. When Max says I will, he does." "That," she added, seeing the opportunity to score a point, "is an advantage of knowing everyone you deal with personally."

Taylor inclined his head in acknowledgement as the phone rang on the desk. Signaling for Taylor not to bother, B.J. rose and answered it.

"Lakeside Inn. Oh, hello, Marilyn. No, I've been tied up this morning." She eased a hip down on the edge of the desk and shuffled through her papers. "Yes, I have your message here. I'm sorry, I just got back into the office. No, you let me know when you have all your acceptances back, then we'll have a better idea of how to plan the food and so on. There's plenty of time. You've got well over a month before the wedding. Trust me; I've handled receptions before. Yes, I know you're nervous. It's all right, prospective brides are meant to be nervous. Call me when you have a definite number. You're welcome, Marilyn. Yes, yes, you're welcome. 'Bye."

B.J. hung up the phone and stretched her back before she realized Taylor was waiting for an explanation. "That was Marilyn," B.J. informed him. "She was grateful."

"Yes, I rather got that impression."

"She's getting married next month." B.J. lifted a hand to rub at the stiffness in the back of her neck. "If she makes it without a nervous breakdown, it'll be a minor miracle. People should elope and not put themselves through all this."

"I'm sure there are countless fathers-of-the-bride who would agree with you after paying the expenses of the wedding." He rose, moving around the desk until he stood in front of her. "Here, let me." Lifting his hands, he massaged her neck and shoulders. B.J.'s protest became a sigh of pleasure. The word *businesslike* floated quietly out of her mind. "Better?" Taylor asked, smiling at her closed eyes.

"Mmm. It might be in an hour or two." She stretched under his hands like a contented kitten. "Ever since Marilyn set the date, she's been on the phone three times a week to check on the reception. It's hard to believe someone could get that excited about getting married."

"Well, not everyone is as cool and collected as you," Taylor remarked as he ran his thumbs along her jawline, stroking his other fingers along the base of her neck. "And, by the way, I wouldn't spread that eloping idea of yours around if I were you. I imagine the inn makes a good profit doing wedding receptions."

"Profit?" B.J. opened her eyes and tried to concentrate on what they had been saying. It was difficult to think with his hands so warm and strong on her skin. "Profit?" she said again and swallowed as her brain cleared. "Oh well . . . yes." She scooted off the desk and out of his

reach. "Yes, usually . . . that is . . . sometimes."
She wandered the room wishing the interlude
in the kitchen had not made her forget who he
was. "It depends, you see, on . . . Oh boy." She
ended on a note of disgust and blew out a long
breath.

"Perhaps you'd translate all that into En-
glish?" Taylor suggested. With a twinge of un-
easiness, B.J. watched him seat himself once
more behind the desk. *Owner to manager*
again, she thought bitterly.

"Well, you see," she began, striving for non-
chalance. "There are occasions when we do
wedding receptions or certain parties without
charge. That is," she rushed on as his face
remained inscrutable, "we charge for the food
and supplies, but not for the use of the
lounge . . ."

"Why?" The one word interruption was followed by several seconds of complete silence.

"Why?" B.J. repeated and glanced briefly at
the ceiling for assistance. "It depends, of course,
and it is the exception rather than the rule."
Why? she demanded of herself. *Why don't I
learn to keep my mouth shut?* "In this case,
Marilyn is Dot's cousin. You met Dot, she's one
of our waitresses," she continued as Taylor remained unhelpfully silent. "She also works here
during the summer season. We decided, as we do
on certain occasions, to give Marilyn the reception as a wedding present."

"We?"

"The staff," B.J. explained. "Marilyn is responsible for the food, entertainment, flowers,
but we contribute the lounge and our time, and,"

she added, dropping her voice to a mumble, "the wedding cake."

"I see." Taylor leaned back in the chair and laced his fingers together. "So, the staff donates their time and talent and the inn."

"Just the lounge." B.J. met his accusatory glance with a glare. "It's something we do only a couple of times a year. And if I must justify it from a business standpoint, it's good public relations. Maybe it's even tax deductible. Ask your C.P.A." She began to storm around the office as her temper rose, but Taylor sat calmly. "I don't see why you have to be so picky. The staff works on their own time. We've been doing it for years. It's . . ."

"Inn policy," Taylor finished for her. "Perhaps I should have you list all the eccentricities of inn policy for me. But I should remind you, B.J., that the inn's policy is not carved in stone."

"You're not going to drop the axe on Marilyn's reception," B.J. stated, prepared for a fight to the finish.

"I've misplaced my black hood, B.J., so I can't play executioner. However," he continued before the look of satisfaction could be fully formed on her face, "you and I will have to have a more detailed discussion on the inn's public relations."

"Yes, sir," she replied in her most wintry voice, and was saved from further argument by the ringing of the phone.

Taylor motioned for her to answer it. "I'll get us some coffee."

B.J. watched him stroll from the room as she lifted the phone to her ear.

When Taylor returned a few moments later, she was seated behind the desk just replacing the receiver. With a sound of annoyance, she supported her chin on her elbows.

"The florist doesn't have my six dozen daffodils."

"I'm sorry to hear that." Taylor placed her coffee on the desk.

"Well, you should be. It's your inn, and they are actually your daffodils."

"It's kind of you to think of me, B.J.," Taylor said amiably. "But don't you think six dozen is a bit extreme?"

"Very funny," she muttered and picked up her coffee cup. "You won't think it's such a joke when there aren't any flowers on the tables."

"So, order something besides daffodils."

"Do I look like a simpleton?" B.J. demanded. "He won't have anything in that quantity until next week. Some trouble at the greenhouse or something. Blast it!" She swallowed her coffee and scowled at the far wall.

"For heaven's sake, B.J., there must be a dozen florists in Burlington. Have them delivered." Taylor dismissed the matter of daffodils with an airy wave.

B.J. gave him an opened mouth look of astonishment. "Delivered from Burlington? Do you have any idea how much those daffodils would cost?" Rising, she paced the room while she considered her options. "I simply can't tolerate artificial flowers," she muttered while Taylor sipped his coffee and watched her. "They're worse than no flowers at all. I hate to do it," she said with a sigh. "It's bad enough having to beg for her jelly, now I'm going to have to beg for her flowers. There's absolutely nothing else I can do. She's got the only garden in town that can handle it." Making a complete circle of the room, B.J. plopped down behind the desk again.

"Are you finished?"

"No," B.J. answered, picking up the phone. "I still have to talk her out of them." Grimly, she set her teeth. "Wish me luck."

Deciding all would be explained in due time, Taylor sat back to watch. "Luck," he said agreeably and finished off his coffee.

When B.J. had completed her conversation, he shook his head in frank admiration. "That," he said as he toasted her with his empty cup, "was the most blatant con job I've ever witnessed."

"Subtlety doesn't work with Betty Jackson." Smug, B.J. answered his toast, then rose. "I'm going to go pick up those flowers before she changes her mind.

"I'll drive you," Taylor offered, taking her arm before she reached the door.

"Oh, you needn't bother." The contact reminded her how slight was her will when he touched her.

"It's no bother," he countered, leading her through the inn's front door. "I feel I must see the woman who, how did you put it? 'Raises flowers with an angel's touch.'"

"Did I say that?" B.J. struggled to prevent a smile.

"That was one of your milder compliments."

"Desperate circumstances call for desperate measures," B.J. claimed and slid into Taylor's Mercedes. "Besides, Miss Jackson does have an extraordinary garden. Her rosebush won a prize last year. Turn left here," she instructed as he came to a fork in the road. "You know, you should be grateful to me instead of making fun. If you'd had your way, we'd be eating up a healthy percentage of the inn's profits in delivery fees."

"My dear Miss Clark," Taylor drawled, "if there's one thing I can't deny, it's that you are a top flight manager. Of course, I'm also aware that a raise is in order."

"When I want a raise, I'll ask for one," B.J. snapped. As she gave her attention to the view out the side window, she missed Taylor's glance of speculation. She had not liked his use of her surname, nor had she liked being reminded again so soon of the status of their positions. He was her employer, and there was no escaping it. Closing her eyes, she chewed on her lower lip. The day had not run smoothly, perhaps that was why she had been so acutely annoyed over such a small thing. *And so rude,* she added to herself. Decidedly, it was her responsibility to offer the olive branch. Turning, she gave Taylor a radiant smile.

"What sort of raise?"

He laughed, and reached over to ruffle her hair. "What an odd one you are, B.J."

"Oh, I know," she agreed, wishing she could understand her own feelings. "I know. There's the house." She gestured as they approached. "Third from the corner."

They alighted from opposite sides of the car, but Taylor took her arm as they swung through Betty Jackson's gate. This visit, B.J. decided, thinking of the silver blue Mercedes and Taylor's elegantly simple silk shirt, should keep Miss Jackson in news for six months. The doorbell was answered before it had stopped ringing.

"Hello, Miss Jackson," B.J. began and prepared to launch into her first thank you speech. She closed her mouth as she noticed Betty's attention was focused well over her head. "Oh, Miss Jackson, this is Taylor Reynolds, the owner of the inn. Taylor, Betty Jackson." B.J. made introductions as Betty simultaneously pulled her apron from her waist and metal clips from her hair.

"Miss Jackson." Taylor took her free hand as Betty held the apron and clips behind her back. "I've heard so much about your talents, I feel we're old friends." Blushing like a teenager, Betty was, for the first time in her sixty odd years, at a loss for words.

"We came by for the flowers," B.J. reminded her, fascinated by Betty's reaction.

"Flowers? Oh, yes, of course. Do come in." She ushered them into the house and into her living room, all the while keeping her hand behind her back.

"Charming," Taylor stated, gazing around at chintz and doilies. Turning, he gave Betty his easy smile. "I must tell you, Miss Jackson, we're very grateful to you for helping us out this way."

"It's nothing, nothing at all," Betty said, fluttering her hand with the words. "Please sit down. I'll fix us a nice pot of tea. Come along, B.J." She scurried from the room, leaving B.J. no choice but to follow. Safely enclosed in the kitchen, Betty began to move at lightning speed.

"Why didn't you tell me you were bringing *him*?" she demanded, flourishing a teapot.

"Well, I didn't know until . . ."

"Goodness, you could have given a person a chance to comb her hair and put her face on." Betty dug out her best china cups and inspected them for chips.

B.J. bit the inside of her lip to keep a grin from forming. "I'm sorry, Betty. I had no idea Mr. Reynolds was coming until I was leaving."

"Never mind, never mind." Betty brushed aside the apology with the back of her hand. "You did bring him after all. I'm positively dying to talk to him. Why don't you run out and get your flowers now before tea?" She produced a pair of scissors. "Just pick whatever you need." She dismissed B.J. with a hasty wave. "Take your time."

After the back door had closed firmly in her face, B.J. stood for a moment, torn between amusement and exasperation before heading towards Betty's early spring blooms.

When she re-entered the kitchen about twenty minutes later, armed with a selection of daffodils and early tulips, she could hear Betty laughing. Carefully placing her bouquet on the kitchen table, she walked into the living room.

Like old friends, Taylor and Betty sat on the sofa, a rose patterned teapot nestled cozily on the low table. "Oh, Taylor," Betty said, still laughing, "you tell such stories! What's a poor woman to believe?"

B.J. looked on in stunned silence. She was certain Betty Jackson had not flirted this outrageously in thirty years. And, she noted with a shake of her head, Taylor was flirting with equal aplomb. As Betty leaned forward to pour more tea, Taylor glanced over her head and shot B.J. a grin so endearingly boyish it took all her will-power not to cross the room and throw herself into his arms. He was, she thought with a curious catch in her heart, impossible. No female under a hundred and two was safe around him. Unable to do otherwise, B.J. answered his grin.

"Miss Jackson," B.J. said, carefully readjusting her features. "Your garden is lovely as always."

"Thanks, B.J. I really do work hard on it. Did you get all that you wanted?"

"Yes, thank you. I don't know how I would have managed without you."

"Well." Betty sighed as she rose. "I'll just get a box for them."

Some fifteen minutes later, after Betty had exacted a promise from Taylor that he drop by again, B.J. was in the Mercedes beside him. In the back seat were the assortment of flowers and a half a dozen jars of jelly as a gift for Taylor.

"You," B.J. began in the sternest voice she could manage, "should be ashamed."

"I?" Taylor countered, giving her an innocent look. "Whatever for?"

"You know very well what for," B.J. said severely. "You very near had Betty swooning."

"I can't help it if I'm charming and irresistible."

"Oh yes, you can," she disagreed. "You were

deliberately charming and irresistible. If you'd said the word, she'd have ripped up her prize rosebush and planted it at the inn's front door."

"Nonsense," Taylor claimed. "We were simply having an enjoyable conversation."

"Did you enjoy the camomile tea?" B.J. asked sweetly.

"Very refreshing. You didn't get a cup, did you?"

"No." B.J. sniffed and folded her arms across her chest. "I wasn't invited."

"Ah, now I see." Taylor sighed as he pulled in front of the inn. "You're jealous."

"Jealous?" B.J. gave a quick laugh and brushed the dust from her skirt. "Ridiculous."

"Yes, I see it now," he said smugly, repressing a grin. "Silly girl!" With this, he stopped the car, and turning to B.J. lowered his smiling mouth to hers. Imperceptibly, his lips lost their teasing quality, becoming warm and soft on her skin. B.J.'s playful struggles ceased, and she stiffened in his arms.

"Taylor, let me go." She found it was more difficult now to catch her breath than it had been when she had been laughing. A small moan escaped her as his lips trailed to her jawline. "No," she managed, and putting her fingers to his lips, pushed him away. He studied her, his eyes dark and full of knowledge as she fought to control her breathing. "Taylor, I think it's time we established some rules."

"I don't believe in rules between men and women, and I don't follow any." He said this with such blatant arrogance, B.J. was shocked into silence. "I'll let you go now, because I don't think it's wise to make love with you in broad daylight in the front seat of my car. However, the time will come when the circumstances will be more agreeable."

B.J. narrowed her eyes and found her voice. "You seriously don't think I'll agree to that, do you?"

"When the time comes, B.J.," he said with maddening confidence, "you'll be happy to agree."

"Fat chance," she said as she struggled out of the car. "We're never going to agree about anything." Slamming the door gave her some satisfaction.

As she ran up the front steps and into the inn, B.J. decided she never wanted to hear the word *businesslike* again.

Chapter Six

B.J. was standing on the wide lawn enjoying the warmth of the spring sun. She had decided to avoid Taylor Reynolds as much as possible and concentrate on her own myriad responsibilities. Unfortunately, that had not been as easy as she had hoped: she had been forced to deal with him on a daily business basis.

Though the inn was relatively quiet, B.J. knew that in a month's time, when the summer season began, the pace would pick up. Her gaze traveled the length and height of the inn, admiring the mellowed bricks serene against the dark pines, the windows blinking in the bright spring sun. On the back porch, two guests were engaged in an undemanding game of checkers. From where she was standing, B.J. could barely hear the murmur of their conversation without hearing the words.

All too soon, this peace would be shattered by children shouting to each other as they raced across the lawn, by the purr of motorboats as they sped past the inn. Yet, somehow, the inn never lost its informal air of tranquility. Here, she mused, the shade was for relaxing, the grass invited bare feet, the drifting snow for sleigh rides and snow men. Elegance had its place, B.J. acknowledged, but the Lakeside Inn had a charm of its own. *And Taylor Reynolds was not going to destroy it.*

You've only got ten days left. He leaves in ten days, she reminded herself. She sighed.

The sigh was as much for herself as for the inn's fate. *I wish he'd never come. I wish I'd never laid eyes on him.* Scowling, she headed back towards the inn.

"That face is liable to turn guests away." Startled, B.J. stared at Taylor as he blocked the doorway. "I think it's best for business if I get you away from here for a while." Stepping forward, he took her hand and pulled her across the lawn.

"I have to go in," she protested. "I . . . I have to phone the linen supplier."

"It'll keep. Your duties as guide come first."

"Guide? Would you please let me go? Where are we going?"

"Yes. No. And we're going to enjoy one of Elsie's famous picnics." Taylor held up the hamper he held in his free hand. "I want to see the lake."

"You don't need me for that. You can't miss it. It's the huge body of water you come to at the end of the path."

"B.J." He stopped, turning directly to face her. "For two days you've avoided me. Now, I'm well aware we have differences in our outlook on the inn."

"I hardly see . . ."

"Be quiet," he said pleasantly. "I am willing to give you my word that no major alterations will be started without your being notified. Whatever changes I decide upon will be brought to your attention before any formal plans are drawn up." His tone was brisk and businesslike even while he ignored her attempts to free her hand. "I respect your dedication and loyalty to the inn." His tone was coolly professional.

"But . . ."

"However," he cut her off easily, "I do own the inn, and you are in my employ. As of now you have a couple hours off. How do you feel about picnics?"

"Well, I . . ."

"Good. I'm fond of them myself." Smiling easily, he began to move down the well worn path through the woods.

The undergrowth was still soft from winter. Beneath the filtered sunlight wild flowers were a multicolored carpet, bright against their brown background of decayed leaves. Squirrels darted up the trunks of trees where birds had already begun to nest.

"Do you always shanghai your companions?" B.J. demanded, angry and breathless at keeping pace with Taylor's long strides.

"Only when necessary," he replied curtly.

The path widened, then spread into the grassy

banks of the lake. Taylor stopped, surveying the wide expanse of lake with the same absorption that B.J. had observed in him earlier.

The lake was unruffled, reflecting a few clouds above it. The mountains on its opposite edge were gently formed. They were not as the awesome, demanding peaks of the West, but sedate and well behaved. The silence was broken once by the quick call of a chickadee, then lay again like a calming hand on the air.

"Very nice," Taylor said at length, and B.J. listened for but heard no condescension in his tone. "A very lovely view. Do you ever swim here?"

"Only since I was two," B.J. answered, groping for a friendly lightness. She wished he would not continue to hold her hand as if he had done so a thousand times before, wished hers did not fit into his as if molded for the purpose.

"Of course." He turned his head, switching his study from the lake to her face. "I'd forgotten, you were born here, weren't you?"

"I've always lived in Lakeside." Deciding that setting up the picnic things was the most expedient way to break the hand contact, B.J. took the hamper and began spreading Elsie's neatly folded cloth. "My parents moved to New York when I was nineteen, and I lived there for almost a year. I transferred colleges at mid-term and enrolled back here."

"How did you find New York?" Taylor dropped down beside her, and B.J. glimpsed at the bronzed forearms which his casually rolled up sleeves revealed.

"Noisy and confusing," she replied, frowning at a platter of crisp golden chicken. "I don't like to be confused."

"Don't you?" His swift grin appeared at her frown. With one deft motion, he pulled out the ribbon which held her hair neatly behind her back. "It makes you look like my adolescent niece." He tossed it carelessly out of reach as B.J. grabbed for it.

"You are an abominably rude man." Pushing back her newly liberated hair, she glared into his smiling face.

"Often," he agreed and lifted a bottle of wine from the hamper. He drew the cork with the ease of experience while B.J. fumed in silence. "How did you happen to become manager of the Lakeside Inn?"

The question took her off guard. For a moment she watched him pour the inn's best Chablis into Dixie cups. "I sort of gravitated to it." Accepting the offered cup, she met the directness of his gaze and realized he would not be content with the vagueness of her answer. "I worked summers at the inn when I was in high school, sort of filling in here and there at first. By the time I graduated, I was assistant manager. Anyway," she continued, "when I moved back from New York, I just slid back in. Mr. Blakely, the old manager, recommended me when he retired, and I took over." She shrugged and bit into a drumstick.

"Between your education and your dedication to your career, where did you find the time to learn how to swing a bat like Reggie Jackson?"

"I managed to find a few moments to spare. When I was fourteen," she explained, grinning at the memory, "I was madly in love with this older man. He was seventeen." She gave Taylor a sober nod. "Baseball oozed from his pores, so I enthusiastically took up the game. He'd call me shortstop, and my toes would tingle."

Taylor's burst of laughter startled a slumbering blue jay who streaked across the sky with an indignant chatter. "B.J., I don't know anyone like you. What happened to the toe tingler?"

Overcome by the pleasure his laughter had brought her, she fumbled for the thread of the conversation. "Oh . . . he . . . uh . . . he's got two kids and sells used cars."

"His loss," Taylor commented, cutting a thin wedge of cheese.

B.J. broke a fragrant hunk of Elsie's fresh bread and held it out to Taylor for a slice of cheese. "Do you spend much time at your other hotels?" she asked, uncomfortable at the personal tone the conversation seemed to be taking.

"Depends." His eyes roamed over her as she sat cross legged on the grass, her soft hair tumbling over her shoulders, her lips slightly parted.

"Depends?" she inquired. He stared a moment at her and she fought not to fidget under his encompassing gaze.

"I make certain my managers are competent." He broke the silence with a smile. "If there's a specific problem, I'll deal with it. First, I like to get the feel of a new acquisition, determine if a policy change is warranted."

"But you work out of New York?" The trend of the conversation was much more to her liking. The tension eased from her shoulders.

"Primarily. I've seen fields in Kansas that looked less like wheat than your hair." He captured a generous handful. B.J. swallowed in surprise. "The fog in London isn't nearly as gray or mysterious as your eyes."

B.J. swallowed and moistened her lips. "Your chicken's getting cold."

His grin flashed at her feeble defense but his hand relinquished its possession of her hair. "It's supposed to be cold." Lifting the wine bottle, Taylor refilled his cup. "Oh, by the way, there was a call for you."

B.J. took a sip of Chablis with apparent calm. "Oh, was it important?"

"Mmm." Taylor moved his shoulders under his cream colored tailored shirt. "A Howard Beall. He said you had his number."

"Oh." B.J. frowned, recalling it was about time for her duty date with Betty Jackson's nephew. Her sigh was automatic.

"My, you simply reek of enthusiasm."

Taylor's dry comment brought on a smile and a shrug. "He's just a man I know."

Taylor contented himself with a slight raising of his brow.

The sky was now an azure arch, without even a puff of cloud to spoil its perfection. Replete and relaxed, B.J. rolled over on her back to enjoy it. The grass was soft and smelled fresh. Overhead, the maple offered a half-shade. Its black branches were touched with young, tender leaves. Through the spreading cluster of trees, dogwoods bloomed white.

"In the winter," she murmured, half to herself, "it's absolutely still here after a snowfall. Everything's white. Snow hangs and drips from the trees and carpets the earth. The lake's like a mirror. The ice is as clear as rain water. You almost forget there's any place else in the world, or that spring will come. Do you ski, Taylor?" She rolled over on her stomach, her elbows supporting her head to smile at him, all animosity forgotten.

"I've been known to." He returned her smile, studying the soft drowsy face, rosy from the sun and the unaccustomed wine.

"The skiing's marvelous here." She tossed back her hair with a quick movement of her shoulders. "Snow skiing's so much more exciting than water skiing, I think. The food at the inn brings the skiing crowd. There's nothing like Elsie's stew after a day on the slopes." Plucking a blade of grass, she twirled it idly.

Taylor moved to lie down beside her. She was too content to be alarmed at his proximity.

"Dumplings?" he inquired, and she grinned down into his face.

"Of course. Hot buttered rum or steaming chocolate."

"I'm beginning to regret I missed the season."

"Well, you're in time for strawberry shortcake," she offered in consolation. "And the fishing's good year round."

"I've always favored more active sports." His

fingers ran absently up her arm, and B.J. tried hard to ignore the pleasure it gave her.

"Well." Her brow creased as she considered. "There's a good stable about fifteen miles from here, or boats for rent at the marina, or . . ."

"Those aren't the sports I had in mind." With a swift movement, he dislodged her elbows and brought her toppling onto his chest. "Are they the best you can do?" His arms held her firmly against him, but she was already captured by the fascination of his eyes.

"There's hiking," she murmured, unaware of the strange husky texture of her own voice.

"Hiking," Taylor murmured, before altering their positions in one fluid motion.

"Yes, hiking's very popular." She felt her consciousness drifting as she gazed up at him and struggled to retain some hold on lucidity. "And . . . and swimming."

"Mmm." Absently, his fingers traced the delicate line of her cheek.

"And there's . . . uh . . . there's camping. A lot of people like camping. We have a lot of parks." Her voice faltered as his thumb ran over her lips.

"Parks?" he repeated, prompting her.

"Yes, a number of parks, quite a number. The facilities are excellent for camping." She gave a small moan as his mouth lowered to tease the curve of her neck.

"Hunting?" Taylor asked conversationally as his lips traveled over her jawline to brush the corner of her mouth.

"I, yes. I think . . . what did you say?" B.J. closed her eyes on a sigh.

"I wondered about hunting," he murmured, kissing closed lids as his fingers slid under her sweater to trace her waist.

"There's bobcat in the mountains to the north."

"Fascinating." He rubbed his mouth gently over hers as his fingers trailed lightly up her flesh to the curve of her breast. "The chamber of commerce would be proud of you." Lazily, his thumb ran over the satin swell. Pleasure became a need as warmth spread from her stomach to tremble in her veins and cloud her brain.

"Taylor." Unable to bring her voice above a whisper, her hand sought the thick mass of his hair. "Kiss me."

"In a minute," he murmured, obviously enjoying the taste of her neck, until with devastating leisure, he moved his mouth to hers.

Trembling with a new, unfamiliar hunger, B.J. pulled him closer until his mouth was no longer teasing but avid on hers. Warmth exploded into fire. His tongue was searching, demanding all of her sweetness, his body as taut as hers was fluid. He took possession of her curves with authority, molding them with firm, strong hands. His mouth no longer roamed from hers but remained to devour what she offered. The heat grew to an almost unbearable intensity, her soul melting in it to flow into his. For a moment, she was lost in the discovery of merging, feeling it with as much clarity as she felt his hands and mouth. Soaring freedom and the chains of need were interchangeable. As time ceased to flow, she plunged deeper and deeper into the all-enveloping present.

His hands took more, all gentleness abandoned. It flashed across the mists in her brain
that beneath the control lay a primitive, volatile
force from which she had no defense. She struggled weakly. Her protests were feeble murmurs
against the demands of his mouth. Feeling her
tense, Taylor lifted his head, and she felt the
unsteady rhythm of his breathing on her face.

"Please, let me go." Hating the weak timbre of
her own voice, she sank her teeth into the lip
still tender from his.

"Why should I do that?" Temper and passion
threatened his control. She knew she had neither the strength nor the will to resist him if he
chose to take.

"Please."

It seemed an eternity that he studied her,
searching the smoky depths of her eyes. She
watched the anger fade from his eyes as he took
in the fair hair spread across the grass, the
vulnerable, soft mouth. Finally, he released her
with a brief, muttered oath.

"It appears," he began as she scrambled to sit
up, "that pigtails suit you more than I realized."
He took out a cigarette and lit it deliberately.
"Virginity is a rare commodity in a woman your
age."

Color flooded her cheeks as B.J. began to pack
up the remains of the picnic. "I hardly see what
business that is of yours."

"It doesn't matter," he countered easily and
she cursed him for his ability to retain his composure so effortlessly while her entire body still
throbbed with need. "It will simply take a bit
more time." At her uncomprehending stare, he

smiled and folded the cloth. "I told you I always win, B.J. You'd best get used to it."

"You listen to me." Storming, she sprang to her feet. "I am not about to be added to your list. This was . . . this was . . ." Her hands spread out to sweep away the incident while her brain searched for the proper words.

"Just the beginning," he supplied. Rising with the hamper, he captured her arm in a firm grip. "We haven't nearly finished yet. I wouldn't argue at the moment, B.J.," he warned as she began to sputter. "I might decide to take what you so recently offered here and now, rather than giving you some time."

"You are the most arrogant—" she began. Her voice sounded hopelessly childish even to her own ears.

"That's enough for now, B.J." Taylor interrupted pleasantly. "There's no point saying anything you might regret." He leaned down and kissed her firmly before helping her to her feet. With an easy swing, he reached for the hamper. B.J. was too dazed to do anything but meekly follow him as he led the way toward the homeward wooded path.

Chapter Seven

Once back at the inn, B.J. wanted nothing more than to disengage her arm from Taylor's grasp and find a dark, quiet hole in which to hide. She knew all too well that she had responded completely to Taylor's demands. Moreover, she knew she had made demands of her own. She was confused by her own reactions. Never before had she had difficulty in avoiding or controlling a romantic interlude, but she was forced to admit that from the moment Taylor had touched her, her mind had ceased to function.

Biology, she concluded, darting Taylor a sidelong glance as they approached the skirting porch. It was simply a matter of basic biology. Any woman would naturally be attracted to a man like Taylor Reynolds. He has a way of looking at you, B.J. mused, that makes your mind go fuzzy, then blank. He has a way of touching you that makes you feel as though you never had been touched before. He's nothing like any other man I've ever known. And *I asked him to kiss me.* Color rose to her cheeks. *I actually asked him to kiss me.* It must have been the wine.

Soothed by this excuse, B.J. turned to Taylor as they entered through the side door. "I'll take the basket back to the kitchen. Do you need me for anything else?"

"That's an intriguing question," he drawled.

B.J. shot him a quelling glance. "I have to get back to work now," she said briskly. "Now, if you'll excuse me?"

B.J.'s dignified exit was aborted by a flurry of activity in the lobby. Curiosity outweighing pride, she allowed Taylor to lead her toward the source.

A tall, svelte brunette stood by the desk, surrounded by a clutter of shocking pink luggage. Her pencil-slim form was draped in a teal blue suit of raw silk. The scent of gardenias floated toward B.J.

"If you'll see to my luggage, darling, and tell Mr. Reynolds I'm here, I'd be very grateful." She addressed these requests in a low, husky voice to Eddie who stood gaping beside her.

"Hello, Darla. What are you doing here?"

At Taylor's voice, the dark head turned. B.J. noted the eyes were nearly the same shade as the exquisite suit.

"Taylor." Impossibly graceful on four-inch heels, Darla glided across the lobby to embrace

Taylor warmly. "I'm just back from checking on the job in Chicago. I knew you'd want me to look this little place over and give you my ideas."

Disengaging himself, Taylor met Darla's glowing smile with an ironic smile. "How considerate of you. B.J. Clark, Darla Trainor. Darla does the majority of my decorating, B.J. manages the inn."

"How interesting." Darla gave B.J.'s sweater and jeans a brief, despairing glance and patted her own perfectly styled hair. "From what I've seen so far, my work is certainly cut out for me." With a barely perceptible shudder, Darla surveyed the lobby's hand hooked rugs and Tiffany lamps.

"We've had no complaints on our decor." B.J. leaped to the inn's defense.

"Well." She was given a small, pitying smile from deeply colored lips. "It's certainly quaint, isn't it? Rather sweet for Ma and Pa Kettle. You'll have to let me know, Taylor, if you plan to enlarge this room." Transferring her attention, Darla's expression softened and warmed. "But, of course, red's always an eyecatcher. Perhaps red velvet drapes and carpeting."

B.J.'s eyes darkened to flint. "Why don't you take your red velvet drapes and . . ."

"I believe we'll discuss this later," Taylor said diplomatically, tightening his hold on B.J.'s arm. Struggling to prevent herself from crying with the pain, B.J. found argument impossible. "I'm sure you'd like to get settled in," she forced out between clenched lips.

"Of course." Darla viewed B.J.'s brief outburst with a fluttering of heavy lashes. "Come up for a drink, Taylor. I assume this place has room service."

"Of course. Have a couple of martinis sent up to Miss Trainor's room," Taylor said to Eddie. "What's your room number, Darla?"

"I don't believe I have one yet." Again using her extensive lashes to advantage, Darla turned to a still dazed Eddie. "There seems to be a small communication problem."

"Give Miss Trainor 314, Eddie, and see to her bags." The sharp command in B.J.'s voice snapped Eddie's daydream, and he scurried to comply. "I hope you find it suitable." B.J. turned her best managerial smile on her new and unwelcome guest. "Please let me know if there's anything you need. I'll see to your drinks."

Taylor's hand held her still another moment. "I'll speak with you later."

"Delighted," B.J. returned, feeling the circulation slowly returning to her arm as he released it. "I'll wait to be summoned at your convenience, Mr. Reynolds. Welcome to the Lakeside Inn, Miss Trainor. Have a nice stay."

It was a simple matter to avoid a private meeting with Taylor as he spent the remainder of the day in Darla Trainor's company. They were closeted in 314 for what seemed to B.J. a lifetime. To boost her ego B.J. decided to phone Howard. They arranged a date for the following evening. *Well, at least Howard doesn't closet himself downing martinis with Miss Glamorpuss*, she thought. Somehow this knowledge was not as comforting as it should have been.

* * *

The dress B.J. had chosen for dinner was black and sleek. It molded her subtle curves with a lover's intimacy, falling in a midnight pool around her ankles, with a gentle caress for thighs and calves. Small pearl buttons ran from her throat to her waist. The high, puritanical neckline accentuated her firm, small breasts and emphasized her slender neck. She left her hair loose to float in a pale cloud around her shoulders. She touched her scent behind her ears before leaving her room to descend to the dining room.

The candle-lit, corner table where Taylor sat with Darla was intimate and secluded. Glancing in their direction, B.J. could not suppress a scowl. There was no denying that they were a handsome couple. *Made for each other,* she thought bitterly. Darla's vermilion sheath plunged to reveal the creamy swell of her breasts. Taylor's dark suit was impeccably cut. In spite of herself, B.J. eyes were drawn to the breadth of his shoulders. She drew in her breath sharply, recalling the feel of his corded muscles now expertly concealed by the fine tailoring, and shivered involuntarily.

Taylor glanced over, his expression undefinable as he made a slow, exacting survey his eyes lingering on the gentle curves draped in the simplicity of unrelieved black. Though her skin grew warm, B.J. met his eyes levelly. Examination complete, Taylor lifted one brow, whether in approval or disapproval, she could not determine. With a brief gesture of his hand, he ordered B.J. to his table.

Fuming at the casual insolence of the command, she schooled her features into tranquility. She wove her way through the room, deliberately stopping to speak with diners along the route.

"Good evening." B.J. greeted Taylor and his companion with a professional smile. "I hope you're enjoying your meal."

"As always, the food is excellent." Taylor rose and pulled up a chair expectantly. His eyes narrowed in challenge. It was not the moment to cross him, B.J. decided.

"I trust your room pleases you, Miss Trainor." she said pleasantly, as she sat down.

"It's adequate, Miss Clark. Though I must say, I was rather taken aback by the decorating scheme."

"You'll join us for a drink," Taylor stated, motioning a waitress over without waiting for B.J.'s consent. She glared at him for a moment before she glanced up at Dot.

"My usual," she said, not feeling obliged to explain this was a straight ginger ale. She turned back to Darla, coating her voice with polite interest. "And what is it about the decorating which took you aback, Miss Trainor?"

"Really, Miss Clark," Darla began as though the matter was obvious. "The entire room is *provincial*, don't you agree? There are some rather nice pieces, I admit, if one admires American antiques, but Taylor and I have always preferred a modern approach."

Fighting her annoyance and an all too unwanted spasm of jealousy, B.J. said sarcastically, "I see. Perhaps you'd care to elaborate on the modern approach for this country bumpkin. I so seldom get beyond the local five and dime."

Dot set B.J.'s drink in front of her and scurried away, recognizing storm warnings.

"In the first place," Darla began, immune to her frosty gray eyes, "the lighting is all wrong. Those glass domed lamps with pull chains are archaic. You need wall to wall carpeting. The hand hooked rugs and faded Persians will have to go. And the bathroom . . . Well, needless to say, the bathroom is hopeless." With a sigh, Darla lifted her champagne cocktail and sipped. "Footed tubs belong in period comedies, not in hotels."

B.J. chewed on a piece of ice to keep her temper from boiling over. "Our guests have always found a certain charm in the baths."

"Perhaps," Darla acknowledged with a depreciating shrug. "But with the proper changes and improvements, you'll be catering to a different type of clientele." She drew out a slim cigarette, giving Taylor a brief flutter of lashes as he lit it.

"Do you have any objections to footed tubs and pull chains?" B.J. asked him, voice precise, eyes stormy.

"They suit the present atmosphere of the inn." His voice was equally precise, his eyes cool.

"Maybe I've got a few fresh ideas for you, Miss Trainor, if and when you pull out your little book of samples." Setting down her glass, B.J. watched from the corner of her eye as Taylor flicked his lighter at the end of his cigarette. "Mirrors should be good on the ceiling in particular. Just a light touch of decadence. Lots of chrome and glass to give the rooms that spacious, symmetrical look. And white, plenty of white as well, perhaps with fuchsia accents. The bed, of course," she continued with fresh inspiration. "A large circular bed with fuchsia coverings. Do you like fuchsia, Taylor?"

"I don't believe I asked for your advice on decorating tonight, B.J." Taylor drew casually on his cigarette. The smoke traveled in a thin column towards the exposed beam ceiling.

"I'm afraid, Miss Clark," Darla commented, spurred on by Taylor's mild reproof, "that your taste runs to the vulgar."

"Oh really?" B.J. blinked as if surprised. "I suppose that's what comes from being a country bumpkin."

"I'm sure whatever I ultimately decide will suit you, Taylor." Darla placed a hand with easy familiarity on his as B.J.'s temper rose. "But it will take a bit longer than usual as the alterations will be so drastic."

"Take all the time you need." B.J. gestured with magnanimity as she rose. "In the meantime, keep your hands off my footed tubs."

The dignity of her exit was spoiled by a near collision with Dot who had been discreetly eavesdropping.

"An order of arsenic for table three . . . on the house," B.J. muttered, skirting around the wide eyed waitress and sweeping from the room.

B.J.'s intention to stalk straight to her room and cool off was undone by a series of small, irritating jobs. It was after ten when the last had been dealt with and she was able to shut the door of her room and give vent to suppressed temper.

"Country bumpkin," she hissed through clenched teeth. Her eyes rested on a William and Mary table. *She'd* probably prefer plastic cubes in black and white checks. Her eyes moved from the dower chest to the schoolmaster's desk and on to the Bostonian rocker and wing chair in softly faded green. Each room of the inn was distinctive, with its own personality, its own treasures. Closing her eyes, B.J. could clearly see the room which Darla now occupied, the delicate pastel of the flowered wallpaper, the fresh gleam of the oak floor, the charm of the narrow, cushioned window seat. The pride of that particular room was an antique highboy in walnut with exquisite teardrop pulls. B.J. could not recall an occasion when a guest who had stayed in that room had done other than praise its comforts, its quiet charm, its timeless grace.

Darla Trainor, B.J. vowed, *is not getting her hands on my inn*. Walking to the mirrored bureau, she stared at the reflection, then let out a long disgusted breath. She's got a face that belongs on a cameo, and mine belongs on a milk commercial, she thought. Picking up her brush, she told herself that these reflections had nothing to do with the problem at hand.

How am I going to convince Taylor that the inn should stay as it is when she's already rattling off changes and giving him intimate smiles? I suppose, B.J. continued, giving her reflection a fierce scowl, *she's not just his decorator*. The kiss she gave him when she arrived wasn't very businesslike. I don't believe for a moment they spent all that time in her room discussing fabrics.

That's no concern of mine, she decided with a strong tug of the brush. But if they think they're going to start steaming off wallpaper without a fight, they're in for a surprise. She put down her brush and turned just as the door swung open to admit Taylor.

Before her astonished eyes, he closed and locked her door before placing the key in his pocket. As he advanced toward her, she could see that he was obviously angry.

"Being the owner doesn't give you the right to use the master key without cause." she snapped, as she backed against the bureau.

"It appears I haven't made myself clear." Taylor's voice was deceptively gentle. "You have, for the time being, a free hand in the day to day managing of this inn. I have not, nor do I desire to infringe upon your routine. However—" He took a step closer. B.J. discovered her hands were clutching the edge of the bureau in a desperate grip. "All orders, all decisions, all changes in policy come from me, and only me."

"Of all the dictatorial . . ."

"This isn't a debate," he cut her off sharply. "I won't have you issuing orders over my head. Darla is employed by me. I tell her what to do, and when to do it."

"But surely you don't want her to toss out all these lovely old pieces for gooseneck floor lamps and modular shelving. The server in the dining room is Hepplewhite. There're two Chippendale pieces in your room alone, and . . ."

The hand which moved from the back of her

neck to circle her throat halted B.J.'s furious rush of words. She became uncomfortably aware of the strength of his fingers. No pressure was applied, but the meaning was all too evident.

"Whatever I want Darla to do is my concern, and my concern only." He tightened his grip, bringing her closer. Now B.J. read the extent of his anger in his eyes. Like two dark suns, they burned into hers. "Keep your opinions to yourself until I ask for them. Don't interfere or you'll pay for it. Is that understood?"

"I understand perfectly. Your relationship with Miss Trainor has overruled any opinion of mine."

"That"—his brow lifted—"is none of your business."

"Whatever concerns the inn is my business," B.J. countered. "I offered you my resignation once, and you refused it. If you want to get rid of me now, you'll have to fire me."

"Don't tempt me." He lowered his hand and rested his fingers on the top button of her bodice. "I have my reasons for wanting you around, but don't push it. I agreed to keep you abreast of any alterations I decide on, but if you persist in being rude to others in my employ, you'll be out on your ear."

"I can't see that Darla Trainor needs protection from me," B.J. remarked resentfully.

"Don't you?" His temper appeared to drift towards amusement as he scanned her face. "A couple of centuries ago, you'd have been burned at the stake for looking as you do at this moment.

Hell smoke in your eyes, your mouth soft and defiant, all that pale hair tumbling over a black dress." Deftly, his fingers undid the top button and moved down to the next as his eyes kept hers a prisoner. "That dress is just puritanical enough to be seductive. Was it accident or design that you wore it tonight?"

With casual ease, he unloosed half the range of buttons, continuing his progress as his gaze remained fixed on hers.

"I don't know what you mean." Yet her traitorous feet refused to walk away. B.J. found herself powerless to move. "I want . . . I want you to go."

"Liar," he accused quietly, his hands slipping inside the opened front of her dress. His fingers traced lightly over her skin. "Tell me again you want me to go." His hands rose, his thumbs moving gently under the curve of her breasts. The room began to sway like the deck of a ship.

"I want you to go." Her voice was husky, her lids felt heavy with a tantalizing languor.

"Your body contradicts you, B.J." His hands claimed her breasts briefly before sliding to the smooth skin of her back. He brought her hard against him. "You want me just as much as I want you." His mouth lowered to prove his point.

Surrendering to a force beyond her understanding, B.J. rested in his arms. His demands increased with her submission, his mouth drawing the response she had no strength to withhold. While her mind screamed no, her arms drew him closer. The warnings to run were lost as his lips moved to the vulnerable skin of her throat, teasing the softness with tongue and teeth. She could only cling and fret for more. Mouth returned to mouth. While his hands roamed, arousing fresh pleasure, hers slipped under his jacket.

With a suddenness that gave her no time for defense, no thought of resistance, he fell deep into her heart. He claimed its untouched regions with the deftness of a seasoned explorer. The emotion brought B.J. to a spinning ecstasy which vied with a crushing, hopeless despair. To love him was certain disaster, to need him, undeniable misery, to be in his arms, both the darkness and the light. Trapped in the cage of her own desire, she would never find escape.

Helpless to do other than answer the hunger of his mouth, submit to the caressing journey of his hands, she felt the sting of emptiness behind her closed lids. Her arms pulled him closer to avert the insidious chill of reason.

"Admit it," he demanded, his lips moving again to savage her throat. "Admit you want me. Tell me you want me to stay."

"Yes, I want you." The words trembled on a sob as she buried her face in his shoulder. "Yes, I want you to stay."

She felt him stiffen and burrowed deeper until his hand forced her face to his. Her eyes were luminous, conquering the darkness with the glimmer of unshed tears. Her mouth was soft and tremulous as she fought the need to throw herself into his arms and weep out her newly discovered love. For eternity, he stared, and she watched without comprehension as his features hardened with fresh temper. When he spoke, however, his voice was calm and composed and struck like a fist on the jaw.

"It appears we've gotten away from the purpose of this meeting." Stepping away, his hands retreated to his pockets. "I believe I've made my wishes clear."

She shook her head in confusion. As her hand lifted to her tousled hair, the opening of her dress shifted in innocent suggestion over creamy skin. "Taylor, I . . ."

"Tomorrow"—she shivered as the coolness of his voice sapped the warmth from her skin—"I expect you to give Miss Trainor your complete cooperation, and your courtesy. Regardless of your disagreement, she is a guest of the inn and shall be treated as such."

"Of course." The hated tears began to flow as pain and rejection washed over her. "Miss Trainor shall be given every consideration." She sniffled, brushed at tears and continued with dignity. "You have my word."

"Your word!" Taylor muttered, taking a step toward her. B.J. streaked to the bath and locked the door.

"Go away!" No longer able to control the sobs, one small fist pounded impotently against the panel. "Go away and leave me alone. I gave you my promise, now I'm off duty."

"B.J., open this door."

She recognized both anger and exasperation in his tone and wept more desperately. "No, go away! Go keep Miss Perfect company and let me alone. Your orders will be carried out to the letter. Just go. I don't have to answer to you until morning."

Taylor's swearing and storming around the room were quite audible, though to B.J. his muttered oaths and comments made little sense. Finally, the bedroom door slammed with dangerous force. In an undignified huddle on the tiled floor, B.J. wept until she thought her heart would break.

Chapter Eight

"Well, you did it again, didn't you?" B.J. stared at her reflection as the morning sun shone in without mercy. *You made a total fool of yourself.* With a weary sigh, she ran a hand through her hair before turning her back on the accusing face in the mirror. *How could I have known I'd fall in love with him?* she argued as she buttoned a pale green cap-sleeved blouse. *I didn't plan it. I didn't want it.*

"Blast," she muttered and pulled on a matching skirt. *How can I control the way he makes me feel? The minute he puts his hands on me, my brain dissolves. To think that I would have let him stay last night knowing all he wanted from me was a quick affair! How could I be so stupid? And then,* she added, shame warring with injured pride, *he didn't want me after all.* I suppose he remembered Darla. Why should he waste his time with me when she's available?

The next ten minutes were spent in fierce self-flagellation as B.J. secured her hair in a roll at the base of her neck. These tasks completed, she squared her shoulders and went out to meet whatever tasks the day brought.

A casual question to Eddie informed her Taylor was already closeted in the office, and Darla Trainor had not yet risen. B.J. was determined to avoid them both and succeeded throughout the morning.

The lunch hour found her in the lounge, conducting an inventory on the bar stock. The room was quiet, removed from the luncheon clatter. She found the monotony soothing on her nerves.

"So, this is the lounge."

The intrusion of the silky voice jolted B.J.'s calm absorption. She whirled around, knocking bottles of liquor together.

Darla glided into the room looking elegantly businesslike in an oatmeal colored three piece suit, a pad and pencil in perfectly manicured hands. She surveyed the cluster of white clothed tables, the postage stamp dance floor, the vintage upright Steinway. Flicking a finger down the muted glow of knotty pine paneling, she advanced to the ancient oak bar.

"How incredibly drab."

"Thank you," B.J. returned in her most courteous voice before she turned to replace a bottle on the mirrored shelves.

"Fix me a sweet vermouth," Darla ordered, sliding gracefully onto a stool and dropping her pad on the bar's surface.

B.J.'s mouth opened, furious retorts trembling on her tongue. Recalling her promise to Taylor, she clamped it shut and turned to comply.

"You must remember, Miss Clark," Darla's triumphant smile made B.J.'s hand itch to connect with ivory skin, "I'm merely doing my job. There's nothing personal in my observations."

Attempting to overcome her instinctive dislike, B.J. conceded. "Perhaps that's true. But, I have a very personal feeling about the Lakeside Inn. It's more home than a place of business to me." She set the glass of vermouth at Darla's fingertip before turning back to count bottles.

"Yes, Taylor told me you're quite attached to this little place. He found it amusing."

"Did he?" Feeling her hand tremble, B.J. gripped the shelves until her knuckles whitened. "What a strange sense of humor Taylor must have."

"Well, when one knows Taylor as I do, one knows what to expect." Their eyes met in the mirror. Darla smiled and lifted her glass. "He seems to think you're a valuable employee. What did he say . . . rather adept at making people comfortable." She smiled again and sipped. "Taylor demands value from his employees as well as obedience. At times, he uses unorthodox methods to keep them satisfied."

"I'm sure you'd know all about that." B.J. turned slowly, deciding wars should be fought face to face.

"Darling, Taylor and I are much more than business associates. And I, of course, understand his . . . ah . . . distractions with business."

"How magnanimous of you."

"It would never do to allow emotion to rule a relationship with Taylor Reynolds." Drawing a long, enameled nail over the rim of her glass, Darla gave B.J. a knowledgeable look. "He has no patience with emotional scenes or complications."

The memory of her weeping spell and Taylor's angry swearing played back in B.J.'s mind. "Perhaps we've at last reached a point of agreement."

"The first warning is always friendly, Miss Clark." Abruptly, Darla's voice hardened, throwing B.J. momentarily off balance. "Don't get too close. I don't allow anyone to infringe on my territory for long."

"Are we still talking about Taylor?" B.J. inquired. "Or did I lose part of this conversation?"

"Just take my advice." Leaning over the bar, Darla took B.J.'s arm in a surprisingly strong grip. "If you don't, the next place you manage will be a dog kennel."

"Take your hand off me." B.J.'s tone was soft and ominous, as the well-shaped nails dug into her flesh.

"As long as we understand each other." With a pleasant smile, Darla released B.J.'s arm and finished her drink.

"We understand each other very well." Taking the empty glass, B.J. placed it under the bar. "Bar's closed, Miss Trainor." She turned her back to recount already counted bottles.

"Ladies." B.J. stiffened and watched Taylor's reflection enter the room. "I hadn't expected to find you at the bar at this time of day." His voice was light, but the eyes which met B.J.'s in the glass did not smile.

"I've been wandering around making notes," Darla told him. B.J. watched her hand rub lightly over the back of his. "I'm afraid the only thing this lounge has going for it is its size. It's quite roomy, and you could easily fit in double the tables. But then, you'll have to let me know if you want to go moody or modern. Actually, it might be an idea to add another lounge and do both, along the lines of your place in San Francisco."

His murmur was absent as he watched B.J. move to the next shelf.

"I thought I'd get a good look at the dining room if the luncheon crowd is gone." Darla's smile was coaxing. "Why don't you come with me, Taylor, and you can give me a clearer picture of what you have in mind?"

"Hmm?" His attention shifted, but the imperceptible frown remained. "No, I haven't decided on anything yet. Go ahead and take a look, I'll get back to you."

Well arched brows rose at the dismissive tone, but Darla remained cool and composed. "Of course. I'll bring my notes to your office later and we can discuss it."

Her heels echoed faintly on the wooden floor. Her heavy perfume scent lingered in the air after she faded from view.

"Do you want a drink?" B.J. questioned, keeping her back to him and her voice remote.

"No, I want to talk to you."

With great care, B.J. avoided meeting his eyes

in the mirror. She lifted a bottle, carefully examining the extent of its contents. "Haven't we covered everything?"

"No, we haven't covered everything. Turn around B.J., I'm not going to talk to your back."

"Very well, you're the boss." As she faced him, she caught a flash of anger in his eyes.

"Do you provoke me purposely, B.J., or is it just an accidental talent?"

"I have no idea. Take your choice." Suddenly, she was struck by inspiration. "Taylor," she said urgently. "I *would* like to talk to you. I'd like to talk to you about buying the inn. It can't be as important to you as it is to me. You could build a resort further south that would suit you better. I could raise the money if you gave me some time."

"Don't be ridiculous." His abrupt words cooled her enthusiasm. "Where would you come up with the kind of money required to buy a property like this?"

"I don't know." She paced back and forth behind the bar. "Somewhere. I could get a loan for part of it, and you could hold a note for the rest. I've some money saved . . ."

"No." Standing, he skirted the bar and closed the distance between them. "I have no intention of selling."

"But, Taylor . . ."

"I said no. Drop it."

"Why are you being so stubborn? You won't even consider changing your mind? I might even be able to come up with a good offer if you gave me time—" Her voice trailed off uncertainly.

"I said I wanted to *talk* to you. At the moment I don't care to discuss the inn or any part of it."

He gripped her arm to spin her around, connecting with the flesh tender from Darla's nails. B.J. gave a cry of pain and jerked away. Taylor loosened his hold immediately, and she fell into the shelves, knocking glasses in a crashing heap on the floor.

"What the devil's gotten into you?" he demanded as her hand went automatically to nurse her bruised arm. "I barely touched you. Listen, B.J., I'm not tolerating you jumping like a scared rabbit every time I get close. I haven't hurt you. Stop that!" He pulled her hand away, then stared in confusion at the marks on her arm. "Good Lord. I didn't . . . I'd swear I barely touched you." Astonished, his eyes lifted to hers, darkened with emotions she could not understand. For a moment, she merely stared back, fascinated by seeing his habitual assurance rattled.

"No, I did it before." Dropping her eyes, B.J. busied herself by resecuring the pins in her hair. "It's just a bit sore. You startled me when you grabbed it."

"How did you do that?" He moved to take her arm for a closer examination, but B.J. stepped away quickly.

"I bumped into something. I've got to start looking where I'm going." She began to gather shards of broken glass, fresh resentment causing her head to ache.

"Don't do that," Taylor commanded. "You'll cut yourself."

Like an echo to his words, B.J. jerked as a

piece of glass sliced her thumb. Moaning in pain and disgust, she dropped the offending glass back into the heap.

"Let me see." Taylor pulled her to her feet, ignoring her struggles for release. "Ah, B.J." With a sigh of exasperation, he drew a spotless white handkerchief from his pocket, dabbing at the cut. "I'm beginning to think I have to keep you on a very short leash."

"It's nothing," she mumbled, fighting the warmth of his fingers on her wrist. "Let me go, you'll have blood all over you."

"Scourges of war." He brought the wounded thumb briefly to his lips, then wrapped the cloth around it. "You will continue to bind up your hair, won't you?" With his free hand, he dislodged pins, clattering them among broken glass. Studying the flushed face and tumbled hair, his mouth lifted in a smile which brought B.J. new pain. "What is it about you that constantly pulls at my temper? At the moment, you look as harmless as a frazzled kitten."

His fingers combed lightly through her hair, then rested on her shoulders. She felt the sweet, drawing weakness seeping through her limbs. "Do you know how close I came to kicking in that foolish bathroom door last night? You should be careful with tears, B.J., they affect men in strange ways."

"I hate to cry." She lifted her chin, terrified she would do so again. "It was your fault."

"Yes, I suppose it was. I'm sorry."

She stared, stunned by the unexpected apology. In a featherlight caress, he lowered his mouth to brush hers. "It's all right . . . It doesn't

114

matter." She backed away, frightened by her own need to respond, but found herself trapped against the bar. Taylor made no move toward her, but merely said, "Have dinner with me tonight. Up in my room where we can talk privately."

Her head shook before her lips could form a refusal. He closed the space between them before she could calculate an escape.

"B.J., I'm not going to let you run away. We need to talk somewhere where we won't be interrupted. You know that I want you, and . . ."

"You should be satisfied with your other acquisitions," she retorted, battling the creeping warmth.

"I beg your pardon?" At her tone, his face hardened. The hand which had lifted to brush through her hair dropped back to his side.

"I'm sure you'll understand if you give it a bit of thought." She lifted her own hand to the sore flesh of her arm as if to keep the memory fresh. His eyes followed her gesture in puzzlement.

"It would be simpler if you elaborated."

"No, I don't think so. Just don't let your ego get out of hand, Taylor. I'm not running from you, I simply have a date tonight."

"A date?" His slipped his hands into his pockets as he rocked back on his heels. His voice was hard.

"That's right. I'm entitled to a personal life. I don't think it's included in my job contract that I have to spend twenty-four hours at your beck and call." Adding salt to her own wound, she continued, "I'm sure Miss Trainor will fill your requirements for the evening very well."

"Undoubtedly," he agreed with a slow nod. Stung by the ease of his answer, B.J.'s ice became fire.

"Well then, that's all decided, isn't it? Have a delightful evening, Taylor. I assure you, I intend to. If you'll excuse me, I've work to do." She brushed by him, only to be brought up short by a hand on her hair.

"Since we're both going to be otherwise engaged this evening, perhaps we can get this out of the way now."

His mouth took hers swiftly, and she could taste his smoldering fury. She made a futile attempt to clamp her lips tight against his. Ruthlessly, his hand jerked her hair. As she gasped in pained surprise he invaded her mouth, conquering her senses one by one. Just as she had abandoned all semblance of resistance, he drew back, his hands moving with slow insistence from her waist to her shoulders.

"Are you through?" Her voice was husky. Despising the longing to feel his mouth again, she forced herself rigid, keeping her eyes level.

"Oh no, B.J." The tone was confident. "I'm a long way from through. But for now," he continued as she braced herself for another assault, "you'd best tend to that cut."

Too unnerved to answer, B.J. rushed from the lounge. She had left dignity to lay with the scattered pieces of glass.

She felt the kitchen would be the quietest sanctuary at that time of day and entered on the pretext of wanting a cup of coffee.

"What did you do to your hand?" Elsie's question was off-handed as she completed the assembly line production of apple cobblers.

"Just a scratch." Frowning down at Taylor's handkerchief, B.J. shrugged and advanced on the coffee pot.

"Better put some iodine on it."

"Iodine stings."

Tongue clucking, Elsie wiped her hands on her full apron before foraging in a small cabinet for medical supplies. "Sit down and don't be a baby."

"It's just a scratch. It's not even bleeding now." Helplessly, B.J. dropped into a chair as Elsie flourished a small bottle and a bandage. "It's nothing at all. Ouch! Blast it, Elsie! I told you that wretched stuff stings."

"There." Elsie secured the bandage with a satisfied smile. "Out of sight, out of mind."

"So you say." B.J. rested her chin on her hand and stared into the depth of her coffee cup.

"Miss Snooty tried to get into my kitchen," Elsie announced with an indignant sniff.

"Who? Oh, Miss Trainor." Throbbing thumb momentarily forgotten, B.J. gave her cook her full attention. "What happened?"

"I tossed her out, of course." Elsie flicked flour from her abundant bosom and looked pleased.

"Oh." Leaning back in her chair, B.J. laughed at the picture of Elsie ordering sophisticated Darla out of her kitchen. "Was she furious?"

"Fit to be tied," Elsie returned pleasantly. B.J.'s grin widened before she could prevent it. "Going out with Howard tonight?"

"Yes." Her answer was automatic, not even

vaguely surprised that communications had delivered this information to Elsie's ears. "To the movies, I think."

"Don't know why you're wasting your time going off with him when Mr. Reynolds is around."

"Well, it keeps Betty Jackson happy, and . . ." B.J. stopped and frowned as the complete sentence seeped through. "What does Taylor . . . Mr. Reynolds have to do with it?"

"I don't see why you're going out with Howard Beall when you're in love with Taylor Reynolds." Elsie's statement was matter-of-factly delivered as she poured herself a cup of coffee.

"I am not in love with Taylor Reynolds," B.J. declared, gulping down coffee and scalding both tongue and throat.

"Yes, you are," Elsie corrected, adding cooling cream to her own cup.

"I am not."

"Are too."

"I am not. I am absolutely not! Just what makes you so smart?" she added nastily.

"Fifty years of living, and twenty-four of knowing you." The reply was smug.

"La de da." B.J. attempted to appear sublimely unconcerned.

"Be real nice if you got married and settled down right here." Ignoring B.J.'s fit of choking, Elsie calmly sipped her coffee. "You could keep right on managing the inn."

"Stick to chicken and dumplings, Elsie," B.J. advised when she had recovered. "As a fortune teller, you're a complete failure. Taylor Reynolds would no more marry me and settle here than he

118

would marry a porcupine and live on the moon.
I'm a bit too countrified and inexperienced for
his taste."

"Hmph." Elsie sniffed again and shook her
head. "Sure does a lot of looking in your direction."

"I'm sure in the vast wisdom you've amassed
in your famous fifty years, you know the difference between a physical attraction and the urge
to marry and settle down. Even in our sheltered
little town, we learn the difference between love
and lust."

"My, my, aren't we all grown up and sassy,"
Elsie observed with the mild tolerance of an
adult watching a child's tantrum. "Finish your
coffee and scoot, I've got a prime rib that needs
tending. And don't worry that bandage off your
thumb," she ordered as B.J. swung through the
door.

Obviously, B.J. decided as she prepared for
her date that evening, I don't project an imposing enough authority figure. She frowned again
as she recalled Elsie dismissing her like a bad
tempered child. A breeze wafted through her
opened window, billowing the curtains and
wafting in the smell of freshly mowed grass.
B.J. shrugged off her black mood. I'll simply
change my image a bit.

She rooted through her closet and pulled out
her birthday present from her grandmother. The
blouse was pure white silk and plunged deep to
cling provocatively to every curve and plane
before it tapered to the narrow waist of sleek
black pants. The slacks continued a loving em-

brace over hips and down the length of shapely legs, molding her shape with the accuracy of a second skin.

"I'm not sure I'm ready for a new image," she muttered, turning sideways in front of her mirror. "I'm not sure Howard's ready either." The thought brought an irrepressible giggle as Howard's pleasantly homely face loomed in her mind.

He had the eyes of a faithful puppy, made all the more soulful by the attempt of a moustache which hung apologetically over his top lip. The main problem, B.J. decided, concentrating on his image, is that he lacks a chin. His face seemed to melt into his neck.

But he's a nice man, B.J. reminded herself. A nice, uncomplicated, predictable, undemanding man. Easing her feet into leather slides, she grabbed her bag and scurried from the room.

Her hopes to slip unseen outside to await Howard's arrival were shattered by a panic-stricken Eddie.

"B.J. Hey, B.J.!" He loped across the lobby and cornered her before she could reach the door.

"Eddie, if the place isn't burning down, hold it until tomorrow. I'm just leaving."

"But, B.J.," he continued, grabbing her hand and ignoring her unconscious search of the room for a tall, dark man. "Dot told Maggie that Miss Trainor is going to redecorate the inn, and that Mr. Reynolds plans to make it into a resort with saunas in every room and an illegal casino in the back." Horrified, his hand clung to hers for reassurance, his eyes pleading behind the thickness of his glasses.

"In the first place," B.J. began patiently, "Mr. Reynolds has no intention of running an illegal casino."

"He has one in Las Vegas," Eddie whispered in confidence.

"Gambling is a prerequisite in Las Vegas, it's not illegal."

"But, B.J., Maggie said the lounge is going to be done in red and gold plush with nude paintings on the walls."

"Nonsense." She patted his hand in amusement as color rose to his cheeks. "Mr. Reynolds hasn't decided anything yet. When he does, I'm sure it won't run to red and gold plush, and nudes!"

"Thank you," Taylor said at her back. B.J. jumped. "Eddie, I believe the Bodwin sisters are looking for you," he added.

"Oh, yes, sir." Face flaming, Eddie shot off, leaving B.J. in the very position she had sought to avoid.

"Well, well." Taylor surveyed her, an encompassing, thoroughly male examination, lingering on the point where her blouse joined above her breasts. "I trust your date has a high boiling point."

She started to snap that Howard had no boiling point at all, but changed her mind. "Do you really like it?" Tossing clouds of hair over her shoulder, B.J. gave Taylor the benefit of a melting, sultry smile.

"Let's say I might find it appealing under different circumstances," he said dryly.

Pleased to observe he was annoyed, B.J. reck-lessly gave his cheek a brief pat and glided to the door. "Good night, Taylor. Don't wait up now." Triumphant, she stepped out into the pink-clouded evening.

Howard's reaction to her appearance caused her ego to soar yet higher. He swallowed, eyes blinking rapidly, and stammered in small, inco-herent sentences the entire distance to town. Finding this a pleasant change from self-assured amusement, B.J. basked in his admiration as she watched the hazy sun sink beyond the hills through the car window.

In town, the streets were already quiet with the mid-week, mid-evening hush which isolates small towns from the outside world. A few win-dows glowed like cats' eyes in the dark, but most of the houses had bedded down for the night like so many contented domestic pets.

At the far end of town where the theater was, there were more signs of activity. Howard pulled into the parking lot with his usual, plodding precision. The neon sign glowed somewhat ludi-crously against the quiet sky. The *L* in PLAZA had been retired for the past six months.

"I wonder," B.J. mused as she alighted from Howard's sensible Buick, "if Mr. Jarvis will ever get that sign fixed or if each of the letters will die a quiet death." Howard's answer was muffled by the car door slam. She was faintly surprised as he took her arm with a possessive air and led her into the theater.

An hour through the feature, B.J. decided Howard was not at all himself. He did not con-sume his popcorn with his usual voracity, nor did he shift throughout the film on the undeniably uncomfortable seats the Plaza offered. Rather, he sat in a glazed-eyed state that seemed almost catatonic.

"Howard." Keeping her voice low, B.J. placed her hand on his. To her surprise he jumped as though she had pinched him. "Howard, are you all right?"

Her astonishment changed to stunned disbelief when he grabbed her, scattering popcorn, and pressed a passionate if fumbling kiss to her mouth. At first, B.J. sat stunned. All other advances by Howard had consisted of a brotherly embrace at the door of the inn. Then, hearing a few snickers from the back of the theater, she wiggled from his arms and pushed against his stocky chest.

"Howard, behave yourself!" She gave an exasperated sigh and straightened in her seat.

Abruptly, Howard gripped her arm and pulled her to her feet, dragging her up the aisle and out of the theater.

"Howard, have you lost your mind?"

"I couldn't sit in there any more," he muttered, bundling her into his car. "It's too crowded."

"Crowded?" She blew an errant curl from her eyes. "Howard, there couldn't have been more than twenty people in there. I think you should see a doctor." She patted his shoulder then tested his brow for signs of fever. "You're a bit warm and not at all yourself. I can get a ride back, you'd better just go home."

"No!" There was no mistaking the vehemence of his tone.

B.J. gave Howard a long, searching stare before settling back uneasily into her seat. Though it was too dark to tell much, he appeared to be concentrating on his driving. He drove rapidly over the winding country road. Soon B.J. was able to distinguish the blinking lights of the hotel.

Suddenly, Howard pulled off the road and seized her. In the beginning, B.J. was more surprised than angry. "Stop it! Stop this, Howard! What in the world has gotten into you?"

"B.J." His mouth searched for hers, and this time his kiss was neither fumbling nor brotherly. "You're so beautiful." His groping hand reached for her blouse.

"Howard Beall, I'm ashamed of you!" B.J. remonstrated, pushing Howard firmly away and sliding toward the car door. "You get home right now and take a cold shower and go to bed!"

"But, B.J.—"

"I mean it." She wrenched open the car door and jumped out. Standing by the road, she tossed back her hair and adjusted her clothes. "I'm walking right back to the inn before you grow fangs again. Consider yourself lucky if I don't say something to your aunt about your temporary bout of insanity." Turning, she began the half-mile hike to the hotel.

Ten minutes later, shoes in hand and muttering disjointed imprecations toward the entire male sex, B.J. panted up the steep hill. The shadowy trees sighed softly in the moonlight. A lone owl hooted above her. But B.J. was in no mood for the beauties of the evening. "You be quiet," she commanded, glaring up at the bundle of feathers.

"I haven't said anything yet," a deep voice answered.

On the verge of screaming, B.J. found a hand over her mouth. Struggling to escape, she found a hard arm gripping her around the waist. "What the—?"

"Out for a stroll?" Taylor inquired mildly, releasing her. "It does seem an odd place to take a walk," he commented.

"Very funny." She managed two outraged steps before he caught her wrist.

"What's the matter? Your friend run out of gas?"

"Listen, I don't need this right now." Realizing she had dropped her shoes in her fright, B.J. searched the ground. "I've just walked a hundred miles after wrestling with a crazy man."

"Did he hurt you?" The grip on her wrist increased, as Taylor examined her more closely.

"Of course not." Tossing back her hair, B.J. let out a sigh of exasperation. "Howard wouldn't hurt a fly. I don't know what came over him. He's never acted like that before."

"Are you really that artless, or am I watching the second feature?" At her baffled expression, Taylor took her shoulders and administered a brief shake. "Grow up, B.J.! Look at yourself, the poor guy didn't have a chance."

"Don't be ridiculous." She shrugged out of his hold. "Howard's known me forever. He's never behaved like this before. He's just been reading too many romances or something. Good grief, I used to go skinny dipping with him when I was ten years old."

"Has anyone bothered to point out that you're no longer ten years old?"

Something in his voice made her raise her eyes to his.

"Stand still, B.J." He spoke in quiet command, and she felt her knees tremble. "I feel like a mountain lion stalking a house kitten."

For a moment, they stood apart, the stars glimmering above their heads, the moon a pale white guardian. Somewhere, a nightbird called to its mate, a plaintive sound. It echoed into silence as she melted in his arms.

She rose on her toes to offer him the gift of her mouth, her sigh of surrender merging with the wind's murmur. Her breasts crushed against his chest as his hands molded her hips closer. For this moment, she was his. Her heart sought no past or future but only the warmth and knowledge of now—the eternity of the present. She moaned with pleasure as his mouth sought the curve of her neck. Her fingers tangled with his dark hair as his mouth met hers again and she opened her lips to his kiss.

Locked together, they were oblivious to the sounds of night; the sigh of wind, the mellow call of an owl and the chirp of crickets. With a harsh suddenness, the inn door opened, pooling them in artificial light.

"Oh, Taylor, I've been waiting for you."

B.J. pulled away in humiliation as Darla leaned against the doorway, draped in a flowing black negligee. Her ivory skin gleamed against

126

the lace. Her smooth, raven hair fell loose and full down her back.

"What for?" Taylor's question was abrupt.

Darla pouted and moved lace clad shoulders. "Taylor, darling, don't be a bear."

Devastated that he should have used her so blatantly while he had another woman waiting, B.J. stooped to retrieve her shoes.

"Where do you think you're going?" Taylor captured her wrist and aborted her quick escape.

"To my room," B.J. informed him with her last vestige of calm. "It appears you have a previous engagement."

"Just a minute."

"Please, let me go. I've done my quota of wrestling for one evening."

His fingers tightened on her flesh. "I'm tempted to wring your neck." Taylor tossed her wrist away as though the small contact was abhorrent.

Turning on bare heels, B.J. rushed up the steps and past a sweetly smiling Darla.

Chapter Nine

B.J. moved her files to her room. There, she determined, she could work in peace without Taylor's disturbing presence. She immersed herself in paperwork and tried to block all else from her mind. The gray, drizzling rain which hissed at her windows set the stage for her mood. Thick, low hanging clouds allowed no breath of sun. Still, her eyes were drawn to the misty curtain, her mind floating with the clear rivulets which ran down the glass. Shaking her head to bring herself to order, B. J. concentrated on her linen supply.

Her door swung open, and she turned from the slant top desk. With sinking heart, she watched Taylor enter.

"Hiding out?"

It was apparent from the set of his mouth that

his mood had not mellowed since her departure the previous evening.

"No." The lifting of her chin was instinctive. "It's simply more convenient for me to work out of my room while you need the office."

"I see." He towered menacingly over her desk, making her feel small and insignificant. "Darla tells me you two had quite a session yesterday in the lounge."

B.J.'s mouth opened in surprise. She could not believe Darla would have disclosed her own behavior so readily.

"I warned you, B.J., that as long as Darla is a guest of the inn, you're to treat her with the same courtesy you show all other guests."

B.J. was astonished. "I'm sorry, Taylor, perhaps I'm dim. Would you mind explaining that?"

"She told me you were inexcusably rude, that you made some comments on her relationship with me, refused to serve her a drink, made yourself generally unpleasant, and told the staff not to cooperate with her."

"She said that, did she?" B.J.'s eyes darkened with rage. She set her pen down carefully and rose despite Taylor's proximity. "Isn't it odd how two people can view the same scene from entirely different perspectives! Well." She stuck her hands in her pockets and planted her feet firmly. "I have news for you—"

"If you've another version," Taylor returned evenly, "I'd like to hear it.

"Oh!" Unable to prevent herself, she lifted her fist to give his chest a small, inadequate punch. His eyes dropped to it in amused indulgence.

"How generous of you. The condemned man is given a fair trial." Whirling, she paced the room in a swirl of agitation, debating whether to give him a verbatim account of her meeting with Darla. Finally, her pride won over her desire to clear herself in Taylor's eyes. "No thanks, your honor. I'll just take the fifth."

"B.J." Taylor took her shoulders and spun her to face him. "Must you constantly provoke me?"

"Must you constantly pick on me?" she countered.

"I wouldn't have said I was doing that." His tone had changed from anger to consideration.

"That's your opinion. I'm the one who's constantly in the position of justifying myself. I'm tired of having to explain my every move, of trying to cope with your moods. I never know from one minute to the next if you're going to kiss me or sit me in the corner with a dunce hat. I'm tired of feeling inadequate, naïve and stupid. I never felt like any of those things before, and I don't like it."

Her words tumbled out in a furious rush while Taylor merely looked on, politely attentive.

"And I'm sick of your precious Darla altogether. Sick of her criticizing every aspect of the inn, sick of her looking at me as though I were some straw-chewing hick from Dogpatch. And, I resent her running to you with fabricated stories, and, I detest your using me to boost your over-inflated ego while she's floating around half-naked waiting to warm your bed. And . . . Oh, blast!"

Her torrent of complaints was interrupted by

the shrill ringing of the phone. Ripping the receiver from its cradle, B.J. snapped into it.

"What is it? No, nothing's wrong. What is it, Eddie?" Pausing, she listened, her hand lifting to soothe the back of her neck where tension lodged. "Yes, he's here." She turned back to Taylor and held out the phone. "It's for you, a Mr. Paul Bailey."

He took the receiver in silence, his eyes still on her face. As she turned to leave the room, his hand caught her wrist. "Stay here." Waiting for her nod of agreement, he released her. B.J. moved to the far side of the room and stared out at the insistent rain.

Taylor's conversation consisted of monosyllabic replies which B.J. blocked from her mind. Frustrated by the inability to complete her outburst, she now felt the impetus fading. Just as well, she admitted with a sigh of weary resignation. I've already said enough to insure the job at that dog kennel Darla mentioned. Blast! She rested her forehead on the cool glass. Why did I have to fall in love with an impossible man?

"B.J." She started at the sound of her name, then twisted her head to watch Taylor cradle the phone. "Pack," he said simply and moved to the door.

Closing her eyes, she tried to tell herself it was better that she leave, better not to be connected with him even as an employee. Nodding mutely, she turned back to the window.

"Enough for three days," he added in afterthought as his hand closed over the knob.

"What?" Thrown into confusion, she turned,

staring with a mixture of grief and bewilderment.

"We'll be gone for three days. Be ready in fifteen minutes." Halting, Taylor's features softened suddenly at her clouded expression. "B.J., I'm not firing you. Give me credit for a bit more class than that."

She shook her head, washed with relief and the knowledge of the inevitable. He started to cross the room, then paused and merely leaned against the closed door.

"That was a call from the manager of one of my resorts. There's a bit of a problem, and I've got to see to it. You're coming with me."

"Coming with you?" Her fingers lifted to her temple as if she could smooth in understanding. "What on earth for?"

"In the first place, because I say so." He folded his arms across his chest and became the complete employer. "And secondly, because I like my managers well rounded. No pun intended," he added, smiling as her color rose. "This is a good opportunity for you to see how my other hotels are run."

"But I can't just leave at a moment's notice," she objected, as her mind struggled to cope with the new development. "Who'll take care of things here?"

"Eddie will. It's about time he had a bit more responsibility. You let him lean on you too much. You let all of them lean on you too much."

"But we have five new reservations over the weekend, and . . ."

"You're down to ten minutes, B.J.," he informed her with a glance at his watch. "If you don't stop arguing, you'll only have the clothes on your back to take with you."

Seeing all of her objections would be over-ruled, she tried not to think of what going away with Taylor would do to her nervous system. *Business*, she reminded herself. *Just business*.

Somewhat annoyed that he was already walking through the door, having taken it for granted that she was going with him, she called after him, "I can't simply pack because you say to."

He turned back, his temper fraying. "B.J."

"You never said where," she reminded him. "I don't know if I need mukluks or bikinis."

A ghost of a smile played on his lips before he answered. "Bikinis. We're going to Palm Beach."

B.J. was to find her surprises were not yet over for the morning. First, her last minute flurry of instructions was cut off by Taylor's order as she was bundled out of the dripping rain and into his car. On the drive to the airport, she mentally reviewed every possible disaster which could occur during her absence. She opened her mouth to enlighten Taylor only to be given a quelling look which had her suffering in silence.

At the airport, she found herself confronted not with a commercial jet, but with Taylor's private one, already primed for take-off. B.J. stood motionless staring at the small trim plane as he retrieved their luggage.

"B.J., don't stand in the rain. Go on up."

"Taylor." Unmindful of the rain which pelted

her, B.J. turned to him. "I think there's something you should know. I'm not very good at flying."

"That's all right." He secured cases under his arm and grabbed her hand. "The plane does most of the work."

"Taylor, I'm serious," she objected, as he dragged her inside the plane.

"Do you get air sick? You can take a pill."

"No." She swallowed and lifted her shoulders. "I get paralyzed. Stewardesses have been known to stow me in the baggage compartment so I don't panic the other passengers."

He rubbed his hands briskly through her hair, scattering rain drops. "So, I've found your weakness. What are you afraid of?"

"Mostly of crashing."

"It's all in your head," he said easily as he helped her off with her jacket. "There's a term for it."

"Dying," she supplied, causing him to laugh again. Miffed by his amusement, she turned away to examine the plush luxury of the cabin. "This looks more like an apartment than a plane." She ran a hand over the soft maroon of a chair. "Everyone's entitled to a phobia," she muttered.

"You're absolutely right." His voice trembled on the edge of laughter. B.J. turned to snap at him but found his smile too appealing.

"You won't think it's so funny when I'm lying in a moaning heap on your shag carpet."

"Possibly not." He moved toward her and she stiffened in defense. Brooding down at her a moment, he searched her wary gray eyes.

"B.J.," he began, "shall we call a moratorium on our disagreements? At least for the duration of the trip."

"Well, I . . ." His voice was soft and persuasive, and she lowered her eyes to study the buttons of his shirt.

"An armed truce?" he suggested, capturing her chin between his thumb and forefinger and lifting her face. "With negotiations to follow?" He was smiling, his charming, utterly disarming smile. She knew resistance was hopeless.

"All right, Taylor." Unable to prevent her own smile from blossoming, she remained still as his finger lifted to trace it.

"Sit down and fasten your seat belt." He kissed her brow with an easy friendliness which left her weak.

B.J. found that the easy flow of his conversation from the moment of take off eased her tension. Incredibly, she felt no fear as the plane soared into the air.

"It's so flat and so warm!" B.J. exclaimed as she stepped off the plane steps and looked around her.

Taylor chuckled as he led the way to a sleek black Porsche. He exchanged a few words with a waiting attendant, accepted the keys, unlocked the door, and motioned B.J. inside.

"Where is your hotel?" she asked.

"In Palm Beach. This is West Palm Beach. We have to cross Lake Worth to get to the island."

"Oh!" Enchanted by roadside palms, she lapsed into silence.

The white, sandy soil and splashes of brilliant blossoms were so far removed from the scenery of her native New England, she felt as though she had entered another world. The waters of Lake Worth, separating Palm Beach from the mainland, sparkled blue and white under the afternoon sun. The oceanside was lined with resort hotels. B.J. recognized the elaborate initials *T.R.* atop a sleek white building which rose twelve stories over the Atlantic. Hundreds of windows winked back at her. Taylor pulled into the semi-circular macadam drive and stopped the car. B.J. narrowed her eyes against the streaming rays of the sun. The archway which formed the entrance was guarded by palms and semi-tropical plants, their tangle of color obviously well planned and scrupulously tended. The lawn spread, perfectly level and unbelievably green.

"Come," said Taylor, coming around to open the door for her. He helped her out of the car and led her inside.

To B.J. the lobby was a tropical paradise. The floor was flagstoned, the walls a half-circle of windows at the front. A center fountain played over a rocky garden, dotted with lush plants and ferns. B.J. saw that the interior was round, an open circle spiraling to the ceiling where a mural emulating the sky had been painted. The effect was one of limitless space. *How different from the cozy familiarity of the Lakeside Inn!* she thought.

"Ah, Mr. Reynolds." Her meditation was interrupted by the appearance of a slender, well dressed man with a shock of steel gray hair and a lean, bronzed face. "So good to see you."

"Paul." Taylor accepted the proffered hand and returned the smile of greeting. "B.J., this is Paul Bailey, the manager. Paul, B.J. Clark."

"A pleasure, Miss Clark." B.J.'s hand was engulfed by a smooth, warm grasp. His eyes surveyed her fresh, slender beauty with approval. She found herself smiling back.

"See to our bags and I'll take Miss Clark up. After we've settled in a bit, I'll get back to you."

"Of course. Everything's quite ready." With another flash of teeth, he led the way to the registration desk and secured a key. "Your bags will be right up, Mr. Reynolds. Is there anything else you'd like?"

"Not at the moment. B.J.?"

"What?" B.J. was still admiring the luxurious lobby.

"Would you like anything?" Taylor smiled at her and brushed a curl from her cheek.

"Oh . . . no, nothing. Thank you."

With a final nod for Bailey, Taylor secured her hand in his and led her to one of the three elevators. They glided up in a cage of octagon glass high above the cluster of greenery.

When they reached the top floor, Taylor moved along the thick carpeting to unlock the door. B.J. entered and crossing the silent plush of ivory carpet, stared down from a dizzying height at the white beach which jutted out into an azure span of sea. In the distance, she could see the churning whitecaps and the flowing grace of gulls as they circled and dove.

"What an incredible view. I'm tempted to dive straight off the balcony." Turning, she caught Taylor watching her from the center of the room. She could not decipher the expression in his eyes. "This is lovely," she said to break the long silence.

She ran a finger over the smooth surface of an ebony bar and wondered if Darla had decorated the room. Grudgingly, she admitted to herself if this were the case, Darla had done a good job.

"Would you like a drink?" Taylor pushed a button cunningly concealed in the mirror tiles on the wall behind the bar. A panel slid open to reveal a fully stocked bar.

"Very clever." B.J. smiled. "Some club soda would be nice," she said, leaning elbows on the bar.

"Nothing stronger?" he asked as he poured the soda over crackling ice. "Come in," he responded to the quiet knock on the door.

"Your luggage, Mr. Reynolds." A red-and-black-uniformed bellboy carried in the cases. B.J. was conscious of his curious gaze and blushed self-consciously.

"Fine, just leave them there." He accepted the tip from Taylor and vanished, closing the door with quiet respect.

B.J. eyed the cases. Taylor's elegant gray sat neatly beside her practical brown. "Why did he bring it all in here?" Setting down her glass, she lifted her eyes. "Shouldn't he have just taken mine to my room?"

"He did." Taylor secured another bottle and poured himself a portion of Scotch.

"But, I thought this was your suite." B.J. glanced around the luxurious room again.

"It is."

"But you just said . . ." She faltered, as her color rose. "Surely you don't think I'm going to—to . . ."

"What did you have in mind?" Taylor inquired with infuriating amusement.

"You said you wanted me to see how one of your other hotels was run, you never said anything about . . . about . . ."

"You really must learn to complete a sentence, B.J."

"I'm not sleeping with you," she stated very positively, her eyes like two summer storm clouds.

"I don't believe I asked you to," he said lazily before he took an easy sip of Scotch. "There are two very adequate bedrooms in this suite. I'm sure you'll find yours comfortable."

Embarrassment flooded her cheeks. "I'm not staying in here with you. Everyone will think that I'm . . . that we're . . ."

"I've never known you to be quite so coherent." His mockery increased her wrath, and her eyes narrowed to dangerous slits. "In any case," he continued unperturbed, "the purity of your reputation is already in question. As you're traveling with me, it will naturally be assumed that we're lovers. As we know differently," he went on as her mouth dropped open, "that hardly matters. Of course, if you'd like to make rumor fact, I might be persuaded."

"Oh, you insufferable, egotistical, conceited . . ."

"Name calling can hardly be considered persuasion," Taylor admonished, patting her head in an infuriating manner. "I assume, therefore, you'll want your own bedroom?"

"As this is off season," B.J. began, gaining a tenuous grip on her temper, "I'm sure there are a surplus of available rooms."

Smiling, he ran a finger down her arm. "Afraid you won't be able to resist temptation, B.J.?"

"Of course not," she said though her senses tingled at his touch.

"Then that's settled," he said, finishing off his drink. "If you're harboring the notion that I'll be overcome by lust, there's a perfectly sturdy lock on your bedroom door. I'm going down to see Bailey; why don't you change and grab some time at the beach? Your room's the second door on your left down that hall." He pointed as he moved to the door and slipped through before she had time to frame a response.

Before lifting her case and beginning to unpack, B.J. thought of at least a half a dozen withering remarks she should have made. However, she soon regained her sense of proportion.

After all, it wasn't every day that she had the opportunity to indulge in such luxury. She might as well enjoy it. Besides, the suite was certainly large enough for both of them.

Slipping into brief tan shorts and a lime green halter, B.J. decided to finish her unpacking later and head for the beach.

* * *

Taylor had certainly made the most of nature's gift, offering a luxury playground with an ocean and sky backdrop. B.J. had seen the huge mosaic tiled pool for those who preferred its filtered water to the sea. On her way to the beach, she glimpsed at the expanse of tennis courts with palms and flowering shrubs skirting about the entrance gate. She had seen enough of the hotel's interior to be certain that Taylor left his guests wanting for nothing.

From the beach B.J. shaded her eyes and studied again the perfection of the imposing resort. It was, she admitted with a sigh, elegantly appealing. As far out of her realm as its owner. *Egg noodles and caviar,* she thought ruefully, reflecting both on the comparison between inn and resort and Taylor and herself. They simply don't belong on the same plate.

"Hello."

Startled, B.J. turned, blinked against the brilliant sun and stared at an even white smile in a bronzed face.

"Hello." Returning the smile with a bit more caution, B.J. studied the attractive face surrounded by thick masses of light, sun bleached hair.

"Aren't you going to give the ocean a try?"

"Not today."

"That's very unusual." He fell into step beside her as she began to cross the sand. "Usually everyone spends their first day roasting and splashing."

"How did you know it was my first day?" B.J. asked.

"Because I haven't noticed you here before,

141

and I would have." He gave her an encompassing and intensely male survey. "And because you're still peaches and cream instead of parboiled.

"Hardly the time of year," B.J. commented, admiring the deep, even tan as he shrugged on his shirt. "I'd say you've been here for some time."

"Two years," he returned, with an appealing grin. "I'm the tennis pro, Chad Hardy."

"B.J. Clark." She paused on the tiled walkway which led to the hotel's beach entrance. "How come you're on the beach instead of the courts?"

"My day off," he explained and surprised her by winding the tips of her hair around his finger. "But if you'd like a private lesson, it could be arranged."

"No, thanks," she declined lightly and turned again toward the door.

"How about dinner?" Chad captured her hand, gently but insistently bringing her back to face him.

"I don't think so."

"A drink?"

She smiled at his persistence. "No, sorry, it's a bit early."

"I'll wait."

Laughing, she shook her head and disengaged her hand. "No, but I appreciate the offer. Goodbye, Mr. Hardy."

"Chad." He moved with her through the archway into the hotel's coolness. "What about tomorrow? Breakfast, lunch, a weekend in Vegas?"

B.J. laughed; such ingenuous charm was hard

to resist. "I don't think you'll have any trouble finding a companion."

"I'm having a great deal of trouble securing the one I want," he countered, "If you had any compassion, you'd take pity on me."

With a rueful smile, B.J. surrendered. "All right, I wouldn't mind an orange juice."

In short order, B.J. found herself seated at an umbrella table beside the pool.

"It's not really that early," Chad objected when she adhered to her choice of fruit juice. "Most of the crowd is straggling in to wash off the sand and change for dinner."

"This hits the spot." She sipped from the frosted glass. Then, gesturing with one slender hand, she glanced around at green fan palms and scarlet blooms. "You must find it easy to work here."

"It suits me," Chad agreed, swirling his own drink. "I like the work, the sun." He lifted his glass and smiled with the half toast. "And the benefits." His smile widened. Before she had the opportunity to draw them away, his hand captured her fingers. "How long will you be here?"

"A couple of days." She let her hand lie limp, feeling a struggle would make her appear foolish. "This was actually a spur-of-the-moment trip rather than a vacation."

"Then I'll drink to spur-of-the-moment trip," said Chad.

The friendly, polished charm was potent, and B.J. could not resist beaming him a smile. "Is that your best serve?"

"Just a warm-up." Returning the smile, his

grip on her hand tightened slightly. "Watch out for my ace."

"B.J."

Twisting her head, she stared up at Taylor, frowning above her. "Hello, Taylor. Are you finished with Mr. Bailey?"

"For the moment." His glance shifted to Chad, drifted over their joined hands and returned to her face. "I've been looking for you."

"Oh?" Feeling unaccountably guilty, B.J. nibbled her lip in a tell-tale sign of agitation. "I'm sorry, this is Chad Hardy," she began.

"Yes, I know. Hello, Hardy."

"Mr. Reynolds," Chad returned with a polite nod. "I didn't know you were in the hotel."

"For a day or two. When you've finished," he continued, giving B.J. the full benefit of a cold disapproving stare, "I suggest you come up and change for dinner. I don't think that outfit's suitable for the dining room." With a curt nod, he turned on his heel and stalked away.

"Well, well." Releasing her hand, Chad leaned back in his chair and studied B.J. with new interest. "You might have told me you were the big man's lady. I'm rather fond of my job here."

Her mouth opened and closed twice. "I am not Taylor's lady," B.J. spurted on her third try.

Chad's lips twisted in a wry grin. "You'd better tell him that. A pity." He sighed with exaggerated regret. "I was working on some interesting fantasies, but I steer clear of treading on dangerous ground."

Standing, he lifted her chin and gave her a rather wistful smile. "If you find yourself down here again without complications, look me up."

Chapter Ten

The emphatic slamming of the suite's door gave B.J. some small satisfaction. Advancing with purpose on Taylor's bedroom, she pounded on his door.

"Looking for me?" The voice was dry.

She whirled around. For a moment, she could only gape at the sight of Taylor leaning against the bathroom door, clad only in a dark green towel tied low over lean hips. His hair fell in tendrils over the lean planes of his face.

"Yes, I . . ." She faltered and swallowed. "Yes," she repeated with more firmness as she recalled Chad's comments. "That was an uncalled for exhibition out there. You deliberately left Chad with the impression that I was your . . ." She hesitated, eyes darkening with outraged impotence, as she searched for the right word.

"Mistress?" Taylor suggested amiably.

B.J.'s pupils dilated with fury. "He at least used the term lady." Forgetting the corded arms and dark mat of hair covering his chest, she stalked forward until she stood toe to toe. "You did it on purpose, and I won't tolerate it."

"Oh really?" Had she not been so involved venting her own anger, B.J. might have recognized the dangerous pitch of his voice. "It appears by the speed with which Hardy lured you into his corner, you're remarkably easy prey. I feel it's my obligation to look out for you."

"Find someone else to protect," she retorted. "I'm not putting up with it."

"Just what do you intend to do about it?" The simple arrogance of the question was accompanied by a like smile which robbed B.J. of all coherency. "If giving Hardy and others of his type the impression that you're my property keeps you from making a fool of yourself, that's precisely what I'll do. Actually," he continued, "you should be grateful."

"*Grateful?*" B.J. repeated, her voice rising. "Your property? *A fool of myself?* Of all the arrogant, unspeakable gall!"

Her arm pulled back with the intention of connecting her fist with his midsection, but she found it twisted behind her back with astonishing speed. Her body was crushed against the hard undraped lines of his.

"I wouldn't try that again." The warning was soft. "You wouldn't like the consequences." His free hand lowered to her hip, bringing her closer as she tried to back away. "Don't do that," he ordered, holding her still and trapped against him. "You'll just hurt yourself. It seems we've broken our truce." His words were light, though she saw the signs of lingering temper in his eyes.

"You started it." Her declaration was half-defiant, half-defensive. She kept her eyes level with sheer determination.

"Did I?" he murmured before he took her mouth.

She was washed by the familiar flood of need. Offering no struggle, she went willingly into the uncharted world where only the senses ruled. His hand released her arm in order to roam over the bareness of her back, and she circled his neck, wanting only to remain in the drifting heat and velvet darkness.

Abruptly, he set her free. She stumbled back against the wall, thrown off balance by the swiftness of her liberation.

"Go change." He turned and gripped the knob of his door.

B.J. reached out to touch his arm.

"Taylor . . ."

"Go change!" he shouted. She stumbled back again, eyes round and wide at the swift flare of violence. He slammed the door behind him.

B.J. retreated to her room to sort out her feelings. Was it injured pride? Or was it rage? She could not for the life of her tell.

The early sky lightened slowly from black to misty blue. The stars faded, then died as the sun still lay hidden beneath the horizon. B.J. rose, grateful the restless night was behind her.

She had shared an uncomfortably polite dinner with Taylor, the elegance of the dining room only adding to the sensation that she had stood aside and watched two strangers go through the motions of dining. Taylor's solicitous and unfamiliar formality had disturbed her more than his sudden seething fury. Her own responses had been stilted and cool. Immediately after dinner she pleaded fatigue and crept off unescorted to pass the evening hours alone and miserably awake in her room.

It had been late when she had heard Taylor's key in the lock, his footsteps striding down the hall to pause outside her room. She had held her breath as if he might sense her wakefulness through the panel. Not until she had heard the muffled sound of his door closing had she let it out again.

B.J. felt no better the next morning. The events of the day before had left her with a lingering sense of loss and sorrow. Though she knew that there was little hope, she had finally acknowledged to herself that she was in love with Taylor. But there was no point thinking about it.

She slipped on her bikini, grabbed a terry robe, and tiptoed from her room.

The view from the wide window in the living room drew her. With a sigh of pleasure, she moved closer to watch the birth of day. The sun had tinted the edge of sea and sky with rose-gold streaks. Pinks and mauves shot through the dawning sky.

"Quite a view."

With a gasp, B.J. spun around, nearly colliding with Taylor whose footsteps had been hidden by the thickness of carpet. "Yes," she returned as their hands lifted simultaneously to brush back the fall of her hair which tumbled to her cheek. "There's nothing so beautiful as a sunrise." Disturbed by his closeness, she found her own words silly.

He was clad only in short denim cut-offs, frayed at the cuffs.

"How did you sleep?" His voice was politely concerned.

She shrugged off his question, evading a direct lie. "I thought I'd take an early swim before the beach gets crowded."

Deliberately, he turned her to face him, while he searched her face with habitual thoroughness. "Your eyes are shadowed." His finger traced the mauve smudges as a frown deepened the angles of his face. "I don't believe I've ever seen you look tired before. You seem to have some inner vitality that continually feeds itself. You look pale and fragile, quite unlike the pigtailed brat I watched sliding into home plate."

His touch was radiating the weakness through her so she stepped back in defense. "I . . . It's just the first night in a strange bed."

"Is it?" His brow lifted. "You're a generous creature, B.J. You don't even expect an apology, do you?"

Charmed by his smile, her weariness evaporated. "Taylor, I want . . . I'd like it if we could be friends." She finished in an impulsive rush.

"Friends?" he repeated as the sudden boyish grin split his face. "Oh, B.J., you're sweet, if a bit slow." Taking both hands in his, he lifted them to his lips before speaking again. "All right, friend, let's go for a swim."

But for gulls, the beach was deserted, a stretch of white pure and welcoming. The air already glowed with the promise of heat and light. B.J. stopped and gazed around, pleased with the quiet and the solitude.

"It's like everyone went away."

"You're not much for crowds, are you, B.J.?"

"No, I suppose not." She turned to him with a lift of bare shoulders. "I enjoy people, but more on a one to one level. When I'm around people, I like to know who they are, what they need. I'm good with small problems. I can shore up a brick here, hammer a nail there. I don't think I'm equipped to construct an entire building the way you are."

"One can't keep a building standing without someone shoring up bricks and hammering nails."

She smiled, so obviously pleased and surprised by his observation that he laughed and tousled her hair. "I'll race you to the water."

Giving him a considering look, B.J. shook her head in reluctance. "You're a lot taller than I am. You have an advantage."

"You forget, I've seen you run. And—" His eyes dropped to the length of shapely legs. "For a small woman, you have amazingly long legs."

"Well." She drew the word out, lips pursed. "O.K." Without waiting for his assent, she streaked across the sand and plunged into the sea, striking out with long strokes.

She was brought up short by hands on her waist. Laughing, she struggled away, only to be caught and submerged in the ensuing tussle.

"Taylor, you're going to drown me," she protested as her legs tangled with his.

"That is not my intention," he informed her as he drew her closer. "Hold still a minute or you'll take yourself under again."

Relaxing in his hold, B.J. allowed him to keep them both afloat. She permitted herself a few moments of ecstasy cradled in his arms as the water pooled around them like a cool satin blanket. The change began like a gradual drizzle as she became more aware of his shoulder beneath her cheek, the possessive hold of the arm which banded her bare waist. Powerless to resist, she floated with him as his lips descended to the sleek cap of her hair, then wandered to tease the lobe of her ear with tongue and teeth before moving to the curve of her neck. His fingers traced the low line of the bikini snug at her hips as his mouth roamed her cheek in its journey to hers.

Her lips parted before he requested it, but his kiss remained gentle, the passion simmering just below the surface. His hand touched and fondled, slipping easily under the barrier of her brief top to trail over the curve of her breast. The water sighed gently as flesh met flesh.

What with gentle caresses, the drifting buoyancy of the sea, and the growing heat of the ascending sun B.J. fell into a trancelike state. Perhaps, she thought, mind and limbs lethargic, she was meant to float forever in his arms. She shivered with pleasure.

"You're getting cold," Taylor murmured, drawing her away to study her face. "Come on." He released her, leaving her without support in the sighing sea. The magic shattered. "We'll sit in the sun."

B.J. started for the shore with Taylor swimming easily beside her.

On the beach, she fanned her hair in the sun while Taylor stretched negligently beside her. She tried not to look at the strong planes of his face, his bronzed, glistening skin.

He told me how it would be, she reminded herself. Right from the beginning. I don't seem to be able to do anything about it and if I don't, I'll end up being just another Darla in his life. Bringing her knees to her chest, she rested her chin on them and stared at the distant horizon. He's attracted to me for some reason, perhaps because I'm different from the other women in his life. I haven't their sophistication or experience and I suppose he finds that appealing and amusing. I don't know how to fight both loving him and wanting him. If it were just physical, I could avoid being hurt. If it were only an attraction, I could resist him.

She recalled suddenly his quick violence of the previous day and realized he was a man capable of employing whatever means necessary to gain an objective. At the moment, she knew he was playing her like a patient fisherman casting his line into calm waters. But ultimately, they both knew she would be captured in his net. Though it might be silk, it would still lead to eventual disaster.

"You're very far away." Sitting up, Taylor

tangled his fingers in her damp hair and turned her to face him.

Silently, she studied every plane and angle of his face, engraving them on both heart and mind. *There is too much strength there,* she thought, rocked by a surge of love. Too much virility, too much knowledge. She scrambled to her feet, needing to postpone the inevitable.

"I'm starving," she claimed. "Are you going to spring for breakfast? After all, I did win the race."

"Did you?" He rose as she pulled the short robe over the briefness of her bikini.

"Yes," she said, "positively." Picking up Taylor's light blue pullover, she held it out. "I was the undisputed winner." She watched as he dragged the snug, crew necked shirt over his head then bent to retrieve the towels.

"Then you should buy my breakfast." Smiling, he held out his hand. After a brief hesitation, she accepted.

"How do you feel about corn flakes?"

"Unenthusiastic."

"Well." Her shoulders moved in regret. "I'm afraid my funds are rather limited as I was hauled to Florida without ceremony."

"Your credit's good." He released her hand and swung a friendly arm around her shoulders. They moved away from the sea.

By mid afternoon, B.J. felt euphoric. There was a new, charming friendliness about Taylor that made her realize she liked him every bit as much as she loved him.

She was given a thorough if belated tour of the

hotel, allowed to wander through the silver and cobalt lounge, linger in the two elegantly stocked boutiques and examine the enormous expanse of the steel and white kitchen. In the game room, she was provided with an endless supply of change as Taylor watched her reckless enthusiasm with tolerance.

Leaning against a machine, he looked on as she steered her computer car to another horrendous wreck. "You know," he commented as she held her hand for another quarter, "by the time you've finished, you'll have spent every bit as much as that dress in the boutique cost. Why is it, you'll take the money for these noisy machines, but you refused to let me buy you that very appealing dress?"

"This is different," she said vaguely, maneuvering the car around obstructions.

"How?" He grimaced as she narrowly missed an unwary pedestrian and skidded around a corner.

"You never said if you worked out the problem," B.J. murmured as she twisted the wheel to avoid a slow moving vehicle.

"Problem?"

"Yes, the one you came down here to see to."

"Oh, yes." He smiled and brushed an insistent wisp from her cheek. "It's working out nicely."

"Oh, blast!" B.J. frowned as her car careened into a telephone pole, flipped through the air and landed with an impressive show of computer color and sound.

"Come on." Taylor grabbed her hand as she looked up hopefully. "Let's have some lunch before I go bankrupt."

On the sundeck above the pool, they enjoyed quiche Lorraine and Chablis. A handful of people splashed and romped in the pale blue water. Toying with the remains of her meal, B.J. stared down at the swimmers and sun bathers. Her gaze swept to include the curve of beach before returning to Taylor. He was watching her, a small secret smile on his lips and in his eyes. She blinked in confused embarrassment.

"Is something wrong?" Battling the urge to wipe her cheek to see if it was smudged, she lifted her glass and sipped the cool wine.

"No, I just enjoy looking at you. Your eyes are constantly changing hues. One minute they're like peat smoke, and the next clear as a lake. You'll never be able to keep secrets; they say too much." His smile spread as her color rose. Her eyes shifted to the golden lights in her glass. "You're an incredibly beautiful creature, B.J."

She lifted her head, her eyes wide in surprise.

With a light chuckle, he captured her hand and brought it to his lips. "I don't suppose I should tell you that too often. You'll begin to see how true it is and lose that appealing air of innocence."

Rising, he maintained possession of her hand, pulling her to her feet. "I'm going to take you to the Health Club. You can get a first hand impression of how this place works."

"All right, but . . ."

"I'm leaving instructions that you're to have the complete routine," he interrupted. "And when I meet you at seven for dinner, I don't want to see any shadows under your eyes."

* * *

Transferred from Taylor's authority to a perfectly shaped brunette, B.J. was whirlpooled, saunaed, pummeled and massaged. For three hours, she was alternately steamed and sprayed, plied with iced fruit juice and submerged in churning water. Her first instinct was to retrieve her clothes and quietly slip out. After finding they had been conveniently cached out of sight, she submitted, and soon found tensions she had been unaware of possessing seeping out of her.

Stomach down on a high table, she sighed under the magic hands of the masseuse and allowed her mind to float in the twilight world of half sleep. Dimly, the conversation of two women enjoying the same wonder drifted across to her.

"I happened to be staying here two years ago . . . so incredibly handsome . . . what a marvelous catch . . . All that lovely money as well . . . The Reynolds empire."

At Taylor's name, B.J.'s eyes opened and her inadvertent eavesdropping became deliberate.

"It's a wonder some smart woman hasn't snagged him yet." An auburn haired woman tucked a bright strand behind her ear and folded her arms under her chin.

"Darling, you can be sure scores have tried." Her brunette companion stifled a yawn and smiled with wry humor. "I don't imagine he's averse to the chase. A man like that thrives on feminine adulation."

"He's got mine."

"Did you see his companion? I caught a glimpse last night and again today by the pool."

"Mmm, I saw them when they arrived, but I

was too busy looking at him to take much notice. A blonde, wasn't she?"

"Um-hum, though I don't think that pale wheat shade was a gift of nature."

B.J.'s first surge of outrage was almost immediately replaced by amusement. So, she decided, if I'm to be Taylor's temporary, if fictional mistress, I might as well hear the opinion of the masses.

"Do you think this one will get her hooks in? Who is she anyway?"

"That's precisely what I attempted to find out." The brunette grimaced and mirrored her companion's position of chin on arms. "It cost me twenty dollars to learn her name is B.J. Clark of all things. Beyond that, not even dear Paul Bailey knows anything. She just popped up out of the blue. She's never been here before. As for getting her hooks in." Elegantly tanned shoulders shrugged. "I wouldn't bet either way. His eyes simply devour her; it's enough to make you drool with envy."

B.J. raised a sceptical eyebrow.

"I suppose," the brunette went on, "huge gray eyes and masses of blond hair are appealing. And she is rather attractive in a wholesome, peaches and cream sort of way."

B.J. rose on her elbows and smiled across the room. "Thank you," she said simply, then lowered her head and grinned into the ensuing silence.

Chapter Eleven

Refreshed and pleased with herself, B.J. entered Taylor's suite, carrying a dress box under her arm. Though she had lost the minor tussle with the sales clerk in the boutique, she remained in high spirits. After her session in the spa, she had returned to the shop. Pointing to the gown of silver silk which Taylor had admired, she was prepared to surrender a large hunk of her bank account only to be told Mr. Reynolds had left instructions that any purchases she made were to be billed to him.

Annoyed by his arrogance, however generous, B.J. had argued with the implacable salesgirl. Ultimately, she had left the shop with the dress in hand vowing to see to the monetary details later.

If, she decided, pouring a substantial stream of bath salts under the rushing water of the tub, she was to portray the image of the mysterious lady from nowhere she was going to dress the part. She lowered herself into hot, frothy water and had just begun to relax when the door swung open.

"So, you're back," Taylor said easily, leaning against the door, "Did you enjoy yourself?"

"Taylor!" B.J. slid down in the tub, attempting to cover herself with the blanket of bubbles. "I'm having a bath!"

"Yes. I can see that, and little else. There's no need to drown yourself. Would you like a drink?" The question was pleasant and impersonal.

Recalling the overheard conversation in the spa, B.J.'s pride rallied. It's time, she decided, to give him back a bit of his own.

"That would be lovely." Fluttering her lashes, she hoped her expression was unconcerned. "Some sherry would be nice, if it's no bother."

Watching his brow lift in surprise, B.J. felt decidedly smug. "It's no trouble," he said as he retreated, leaving the door ajar. She prayed fervently the bubbles would not burst until she had a chance to leave the tub and slip into her robe.

"Here you are." Reentering, Taylor handed her a small glass shimmering with golden liquid.

B.J. gave him a smile and sipped. "Thanks. I'll be finished soon if you want the bath."

"Don't rush," he returned, delighted to see her coolness had somewhat rattled him, "I'll use the other."

"Suit yourself," she said agreeably, making sure her shrug was mild and did little to disturb her peaceful waters. Relieved that the door closed behind him, B.J. expelled a long breath and set the remains of her drink on the edge of the tub.

For a full five minutes, B.J. stared at her reflection in the full-length mirror. Silver silk draped crossways over the curve of each breast, narrowing to thin straps over her shoulders before continuing down her sides to leave her back bare to the waist. The skirt fell straight over her slender hips and legs, one side slit to mid-thigh. She had piled her hair in a loose knot on top of her head, allowing a few curling tendrils to escape and frame her face.

B.J. found the stranger in the mirror intimidating. With a flash of intuition, she knew B.J. Clark could not live up to the promises hinted at by the woman in the glass.

"Almost ready?" Taylor's knock and question jolted her out of her reverie.

"Yes, just coming." Shaking her head, she gave the reflection a reassuring smile. "It's just a dress," she reminded both B.J. Clarks and turned from the mirror.

Taylor's hand paused midway in the action of pouring pre-dinner drinks. He lifted his cigarette to his lips, inhaling slowly as he surveyed B.J.'s entrance. "Well," he said as she hesitated, "I see you bought it after all."

"Yes." With a surge of confidence, she crossed the room to join him. "As a woman of ill fame I felt my wardrobe inadequate."

"Care to elaborate?" He handed B.J. a delicate glass.

She accepted automatically. "Just a conversation I overheard in the spa." Her eyes lit with amusement, she set her glass on the bar. "Oh, Taylor, it was funny. I'm sure you have no idea how ardently your . . . ah . . . affairs are monitored." Describing her afternoon at the spa, she was unable to suppress her giggles.

"I can't tell you how it boosts the ego to be envied and touted as a woman of mystery! I certainly hope it's not discovered that I'm a hotel manager from Lakeside, Vermont. It would spoil it."

"No one would believe it anyway." He did not appear to be amused by her story as, frowning, he sipped at his drink.

Confused by his expression, B.J. asked, "Don't you like the dress after all?"

"I like it." He took her hand, the smile at last taking command of his mouth. "Obviously, we'll have to have champagne. You look much too elegant for anything else."

They began their meal with oysters Rockefeller and champagne. Their table sat high in the double level dining room, in front of a wide wall aquarium. As the London broil was served, B.J. sipped at her wine and glanced around the room.

"This is a lovely place, Taylor." She gestured with a fine-boned hand to encompass the entire resort.

"It does the job." He spoke with the smooth confidence of one who knew the worth of his possessions.

"Yes, it certainly does. It runs beautifully. The

staff is efficient and discreet, almost to the point of being invisible. You hardly know they're there, yet everything's perfect. I suppose it's elbow to elbow in here during the winter."

With a movement of his shoulders, he followed her gaze. "I try to avoid hitting the resorts during the heavy season."

"Our summer season will begin in a few weeks," she began, only to find her hand captured and her glass replenished with champagne.

"I've managed to keep you from bringing up the inn all day; let's see if we can finish the evening without it. When we get back tomorrow, we can talk about vacancies and cancellations. I don't discuss business when I'm having dinner with a beautiful woman."

B.J. smiled and surrendered. If only one evening remained of the interlude, she wanted to savor each moment.

"What do you discuss over dinner with a beautiful woman?" she countered, buoyed by the wine.

"More personal matters." His finger traced the back of her hand. "The way her voice flows like an easy river, the way her smile touches her eyes before it moves her mouth, the way her skin warms under my hand." With a low laugh, he lifted her hand, lips brushing the inside of her wrist.

Glancing up warily, B.J. asked, "Taylor, are you making fun of me?"

"No." His voice was gentle. "I have no intention of making fun of you, B.J."

Satisfied with his answer, she smiled and

allowed him to lead the conversation into a lighter vein.

Flickering candles, the muted chink of crystal and silver, the low murmur of voices, Taylor's eyes meeting hers—it was an evening B.J. knew she would always remember.

"Let's go for a walk." Taylor rose and pulled back her chair. "Before you fall asleep in your champagne." Hand in hand they walked to the beach.

They walked in silence, enjoying each other and the night. Merging with the aroma of the sea and the night was the tenuous scent of orange blossoms. B.J. knew the fragrance would be forever melded with her memory of the man whose hand lay warm and firm over hers. Would she ever look at the moon again without thinking of him? Ever walk beneath the stars without remembering? Ever draw a breath without longing for him?

Tomorrow, she reflected, it would be business as usual, and a handful of days after, he would be gone. Only a name on a letterhead. Still, she would have the inn, she reminded herself. He'd said no more about changes. She'd have her home and her work and her memories, and that was much more than some ever had.

"Cold?" Taylor asked, and she shivered, afraid he had read her mind. "You're trembling." His arm slipped around her shoulders, bringing aching warmth. "We'd better go back."

Mutely, she nodded and forced tomorrows out of her mind. Relaxing, she felt the remnants of champagne mist pleasurably in her head.

"Oh, Taylor," she whispered as they crossed

the lobby. "That's one of the women from the spa this afternoon." She inclined her head toward the brunette watching them with avid interest.

"Hmm." Taylor pushed the button for the glass enclosed elevator.

"Do you think I should wave?" B.J. asked before Taylor pulled her inside.

"No, I've a better idea."

Before she realized his intent, he had her gathered into his arms, silencing her protest with a mind-spinning kiss. Releasing her, he grinned down at the openly staring brunette.

B.J. turned to Taylor as the door of the suite shut behind him. "Really, Taylor, it's a crime I haven't a lurid past she could dig up."

"It's perfectly all right, she'll invent one for you. Want a brandy?" He moved to the bar and released the concealing panel.

"No, my nose is already numb."

"I see; is that a congenital condition?"

"It is," she stated, sliding onto a bar stool, "my gauge for the cautious consumption of liquor. When my nose gets numb, I've already had one more than my limit."

"I see." Turning, he poured amber liquid into a solitary snifter. "Obviously, my plans to ply you with liquor is doomed to fail."

"I'm afraid so."

"What's your weakness, B.J.?" The question was so unexpected she was caught unaware. *You*, she almost answered but caught herself in time. "I'm a pushover for soft lights and quiet music."

"Is that so?"

Magically, the lights lowered and music whispered through the room.

"How did you do that?"

He rounded the bar and stood in front of her. "There's a panel in back of the bar."

"The wonders of technology." Nerves prickling, she tensed like a cornered cat when his hand took her arm.

"I want to dance with you." He drew her to her feet. "Take the pins out of your hair. It smells like wildflowers; I want to feel it in my hands."

"Taylor, I . . ."

"Ssh." Slowly, he took out the pins until her hair tumbled free over her shoulders. Then, his fingers combed through the length of it before he gathered her close in his arms.

He moved gently to the music, keeping her molded against him. Her tension flowed away, replaced by a sleepy excitement. Her cheek rested naturally in the curve of his shoulder, as if they had danced countless times before, would dance countless times again.

"Are you going to tell me what B.J. stands for?" he murmured against her ear.

"No one knows," she responded hazily as his fingers followed the tingling delight along her bare skin. "Even the F.B.I. is baffled."

"I suppose I'll have to get it from your mother."

"She doesn't remember." She sighed and snuggled closer.

"How do you sign official papers?" His hand caressed the small of her back.

"Just B.J., I always use B.J."

"On a passport?"

She shrugged, her lips unconsciously brushing his neck, her cheek nuzzling the masculine roughness of his chin. "I haven't got one. I've never needed one."

"You need one to fly to Rome."

"Yes, I'll make sure I have one the next time I do. But I'd sign it Bea Jay." She grinned, knowing he would not realize she had just answered his question. She lifted her face to smile at him and found her lips captured in a gentle, teasing kiss.

"B.J.," he murmured and drew her away before her lips were satisfied. "I want . . ."

"Kiss me again, Taylor." Sweet and heavy, love lay on her. "Really kiss me," she whispered, shutting out the voice of reason. Her eyes fluttered closed as she urged his mouth back to hers.

He said her name again, the words soft on the lips which clung to his in silent request. With a low groan, he crushed her against him.

He swept her feet off the floor as his mouth took hers with unbridled hunger. In dizzying circles, the room whirled as she felt herself lowered to the thick plush of carpet. Unrestrained, his mouth savaged the yielding softness of hers, tongue claiming the sweet moistness. His hand pushed aside the thin silk of her bodice, seeking and finding the smooth promise beneath, his fingers warm and sure. Searching for more, his mouth and hands roamed over her, finding heat beneath the cool silk, fingers trailing up the slit in her skirt until they captured the firm flesh of her thigh.

Tossed on the turbulent waves of love and

need, B.J. responded with a burst of fire. His possession of her mouth and flesh was desperate. She answered by instinct, moving with a woman's hidden knowledge as he took with insatiable appetite the fruits she offered. Her own hands, no longer shy, found their way under his jacket to explore the hard ripple of muscles of his back and shoulders, half-terrified, half-delighting in their strength. From the swell and valley of her breasts, his mouth traveled, burning, tantalizing, to burrow against her neck. Her own lips sought to discover his taste and texture, to assuage her new and throbbing hunger.

His loving had lost all gentleness, his mouth and hands now bringing painful excitement. Her fragile innocence began to dissolve with the ancient cravings of womanhood. B.J. began to tremble with fear and anticipation.

Taylor's mouth lifted from the curve of her neck, and he stared into the eyes cloudy with desire and uncertainty. Abruptly he rose and pulled her to her feet. "Go to bed," he commanded shortly. Turning to the bar, he poured another brandy.

Dazed by the abruptness of the rejection, B.J. stood frozen.

"Didn't you hear me? I said go to bed." Downing half his brandy, Taylor pulled out a cigarette.

"Taylor, I don't understand. I thought . . ." A hand lifted to push at her hair, her eyes liquid and pleading. "I thought you wanted me."

"I do." He drew deep on his cigarette. "Now, go to bed."

"Taylor." The fury in his eyes caused her to flinch.

"Just get out of here before I forget all the rules."

B.J. straightened her shoulders and swallowed her tears. "You're the boss." She ignored the swift flame of temper in his eyes and plunged on. "But I want you to know, what I offered you tonight was a one-time deal. I'll never willingly go into your arms again. From now on, the only thing between you and me is the Lakeside Inn."

"We'll leave it at that for now," he said in curt agreement as he turned away and poured another drink. "Just go to bed."

B.J. ran from the room and turned the lock on her door with an audible click.

Chapter Twelve

B.J. threw herself into the inn's routine like a bruised child returning to a mother's arms. She and Taylor had flown from Florida to Vermont in almost total silence, he working on his papers while she had buried herself in a magazine. Avoiding Taylor for the next two days was easy. He made no effort to see her. Annoyance made hurt more tolerable. B.J. worked with dedication to construct a wall of resentment to shield the emptiness she would experience when he left both the inn and her.

Furthering her resentment was the stubborn presence of Darla Trainor. Although B.J. observed Taylor was not often in her company, her mere existence rubbed the sore of wounded pride. Seeing Darla was a constant reminder of B.J.'s uncomfortable and confusing relationship with Taylor.

B.J. knew she could not have mistaken the desire he had felt for her the last night in Florida. She concluded, watching Darla's sensuous elegance, that he had ultimately been disappointed in her lack of experience in the physical demands of love.

Wanting to avoid any unnecessary contact with Taylor, B.J. established her office in her room for the duration of his stay. Buried to her elbows in paperwork one afternoon, she jumped and scattered receipts as the quiet afternoon was shattered by screams and scrambling feet above her head. Racing to the third floor, B.J. followed the sounds into 314. For a moment she could only stand in the doorway and gape at the tableau. In the center of the braid rug, Darla Trainor was engaged in a major battle with one of the housemaids. A helpless Eddie was caught in the middle, his pleas for peace ignored.

"Ladies, ladies, please." Taking her life in her hands, B.J. plunged into the thick of battle and attempted to restore order. Hands and mixed accusations flew. "Louise, Miss Trainor is a guest! What's gotten into you?" She tugged, without success, on the housemaid's arm, then switched her attention to Darla. "Please, stop shouting, I can't understand." Frustrated because she was shouting herself, B.J. lowered her voice and tried to pull Darla away. "Please, Miss Trainor, she's half your size and twice your age. You'll hurt her."

"Take your hands off me!" Darla flung out an arm, and by accident or design, her fist connected, sending B.J. sprawling against the bedpost.

170

The light shattered into fragments, then smothered with darkness as she slid gently to the floor.

"B.J." A voice called from down a long tunnel. B.J. responded with a moan and allowed her eyes to open into slits. "Lie still," Taylor ordered. Gingerly, she permitted her eyes to open further and focused on his lean features. He was leaning over her, his face lined with concern while he stroked the hair away from her forehead.

"What happened?" She ignored his command and attempted to sit up. Taylor pushed her back against the pillow.

"That's precisely what I want to know." As he glanced around, B.J. followed his gaze. Eddie sat on a small settee with his arm around a sniffling Louise. Darla stood by the window, her profile etched in indignation.

"Oh." Memory clearing, B.J. let out a long breath and shut her eyes. Unconsciousness, she decided, had its advantages. "The three of them were wrestling in the middle of the room. I'm afraid I got in the path of Miss Trainor's left hook."

The hand stroking her cheek stopped as Taylor's fingers tensed against her skin. "She hit you?"

"It was an accident, Taylor." Darla interrupted B.J.'s response, her eyes shining with regret and persecution. "I was simply trying to take these tacky curtains down when this . . . this maid"—she gestured regally toward Louise—"this maid comes in and begins shouting and pulling on me. Then he's shouting—" She fluttered a hand toward Eddie before passing it

171

across her eyes. "Then Miss Clark appears from nowhere, and she begins pulling and shouting. It was a dreadful experience." With a long, shuddering sigh, Darla appeared to collect herself. "I only tried to push her away. She had no business coming into my room in the first place. None of these people belong in my room."

"She had no business trying to take down those curtains," Louise chimed in, wringing Eddie's handkerchief. She waved the soggy linen until all eyes shifted to the window in question. The white chintz hung drunkenly against the frame. "She said they were out-of-date and impractical like everything else in this place. I washed those curtains myself two weeks ago." Louise placed a hand on her trembling bosom. "I was not going to have her soiling them. I asked her very nicely to stop."

"Nicely?" Darla exploded. "You attacked me."

"I only attacked her," Louise countered with dignity," when she wouldn't come down. B.J., she was standing on the Bentwood chair. Standing on it!" Louise buried her face in Eddie's shoulder, unable to go on.

"Taylor." Tucking an errant lock behind her ear, Darla moved toward him, blinking moist eyes. "You aren't going to allow her to speak to me that way, are you? I want her fired. She might have injured me. She's unstable." Darla placed a hand on his arm as the first tear trembled on her lashes.

Infuriated by the display of helpless femininity, B.J. rose. She ignored both Taylor's restraining hand and the throbbing in her head. "Mr. Reynolds, am I still manager of this inn?"

"Yes, Miss Clark."

B.J. heard the annoyance in his voice and added it to her list of things to ignore. "Very well. Miss Trainor, it falls under my jurisdiction as manager of the inn to oversee all hirings and firings. If you wish to lodge a formal complaint, please do so in writing to my attention. In the meantime, I should warn you that you will be held responsible for any damages done to the furnishings of your room. You should know, as well, that the inn will stand behind Louise in this matter."

"Taylor." Nearly sputtering with rage, Darla turned back to him. "You're not going to allow this?"

"Mr. Reynolds," B.J. interrupted, wishing for a bottle of aspirin and oblivion. "Perhaps you'll take Miss Trainor to the lounge for a drink, and we can discuss this matter later."

After a brief study, Taylor nodded. "All right, we'll talk later. Rest in your room for the remainder of the day. I'll see you're not disturbed."

B.J. accepted the display of gratitude and sympathy by both Eddie and Louise before trudging down to her room. Stepping over scattered papers, she secured much needed aspirin then curled up on the quilt of her bed. Dimly, she heard the door open and felt a hand brush through her hair. The grip of sleep was too strong, and she could not tell if the elusive kiss on her mouth was dream or reality.

When she woke up the throbbing had decreased to a negligible ache. Sitting up, B.J. stared at the neat stack of papers on her desk. Maybe it was a dream, she mused, confused by the lack of disorder on her floor. She touched the back of her head and winced as her fingers contacted with a small lump. Maybe I picked them up and don't remember. It's always the mediator who gets clobbered, she thought in disgust, and prepared to go downstairs to confront Taylor. In the lobby, she came upon Eddie, Maggie and Louise in a heated, low-voiced debate. With a sigh, she moved towards them to restore order.

"Oh, B.J." Maggie started with comical guilt. "Mr. Reynolds said you weren't to be disturbed. How are you feeling? Louise said that Miss Trainor gave you a nasty lump."

"It's nothing." She glanced from one solemn face to the next. She moved her shoulders in resignation. "All right, what's the problem?"

The question produced a jumble of words from three different tongues. Pampering her still aching head, B.J. held up a hand for silence. "Eddie," she decided, choosing at random.

"It's about the architect," he began, and she raised her brows in puzzlement.

"What architect?"

"The one who was here when you were in Florida. Only we didn't know he was an architect. Dot thought he was an artist because he was always walking around with a pad and pencil and making drawings."

Resigning herself to a partially coherent story, B.J. prompted, "Drawings of what?"

"Of the inn," Eddie announced with a flourish. "But he wasn't an artist."

"He was an architect," Maggie interrupted,

174

unable to maintain her silence. Eddie shot her a narrowed-eyed frown.

"And how do you know he was an architect?" After asking, B.J. wondered why it mattered. Her wandering attention was soon drawn back with a jolt.

"Because Louise heard Mr. Reynolds talking to him on the phone."

B.J.'s gaze shifted to the housemaid as a hollow feeling grew in the pit of her stomach. "How did you hear, Louise?"

"I wasn't eavesdropping," she claimed with dignity, then amended as B.J. raised her brows. "Well, not really, until I heard him talking about the inn. I was going to dust the office, and since Mr. Reynolds was on the phone, I waited outside. When I heard him say something about a new building, and he said the man's name, Fletcher, I remembered Dot talking about this man named Fletcher making sketches of the inn." She gave the group a small smile in self-reward for her memory. "Anyway, they talked awhile, technical sort of things about dimensions and timber. Then Mr. Reynolds said how he appreciated the Fletcher person not letting on he was an architect until he had everything settled."

"B.J.," Eddie began urgently, grabbing her arm. "Do you think he's going to remodel the inn after all? Do you think he's going to let us all go?"

"No." Feeling her head increase its throbbing, B.J. repeated more emphatically, "No, it's just some mix up, I'll see about it. Now, you all go back to work and don't spread this around anymore."

"It's no mix up." Darla glided over to the group.

"I told you three to go back to work," B.J. ordered in a voice which they recognized as indisputable. They dispersed, waiting until a safe distance before murmuring among themselves. "If you'll pardon me, Miss Trainor, I'm busy."

"Yes, Taylor's quite anxious to see you."

Cursing herself, B.J. nibbled at the bait. "Is he?"

"Oh, yes. He's ready to tell you about his plans for this little place. It's quite a challenge." She surveyed the lobby with the air of one planning a siege.

"What exactly do you know of his plans?" B.J. demanded.

"You didn't really think he intended to leave this place in this condition simply because you want him to?" With a light laugh, Darla brushed away a fictional speck of dust from her vivid blue blouse. "Taylor is much too practical for grand gestures. Though, he might keep you on in some minor capacity once the alterations are complete. You're hardly qualified to manage one of his resorts, but he does seem to think you have some ability. Of course, if I were you, I'd pack up and bow out now to spare myself the humiliation."

"Are you saying," B.J. began, spacing words with great care, "that Taylor has made definite plans to convert the inn into a resort?"

"Well, of course." Darla smiled indulgently. "He'd hardly need me and an architect otherwise, would he? I wouldn't worry. I'm sure he'll keep the bulk of your staff on, at least temporarily."

With a final smile, Darla turned and left B.J. staring at her retreating back.

After the first flow of despair, fury bubbled. She took the steps two at a time and slammed into her room. Minutes later, she sped out again, taking stairs in a headlong flight and stomping into the office unannounced.

"B.J." Rising from the desk, Taylor studied her furious face. "What are you doing out of bed?"

For an answer, she slammed the paper on his desk. He lifted it, scanning her resignation. "It seems we've been through this before."

"You gave me your word." Her voice trembled at the breach of trust but she lifted her chin. "You can tear that one up too, but it won't change anything. Find yourself a new patsy, Mr. Reynolds. I quit!"

Streaking from the room, she collided bodily with Eddie, brushed him aside and rushed up the stairs. In her room, she pulled out her cases and began to toss articles in them at random. Clothing, cosmetics, knick-knacks, whatever was close at hand was dumped, until the first case overflowed.

She stopped her frantic activities to whirl around at the metallic click of the lock. The door opened to admit Taylor.

"Get out!" she commanded, wishing fleetingly she was big enough to toss him out. "This is my room until I leave."

"You're making one beautiful mess," he observed calmly. "You might as well stop that, you're not going anywhere."

"Yes, I am." She caught herself before she tossed her asparagus fern among her lingerie. "I'm leaving just as fast as I can pack. Not only is working for you intolerable, but being under the same roof is more than I can stand. You promised!" She spun to face him, cursing the mist which clouded her eyes. "I believed you. I trusted you. How could I have been so stupid! There's no way I could have prevented you once you'd made your decision, and I would have adjusted somehow. You could have been honest with me."

Tears were spilling over with more speed than she could blink them away, and impatiently she brushed at them with the back of her hand. "Oh!" She spun away to pull pictures from the wall. "I wish I were a man!"

"If you were a man, we'd have had no problem to begin with. If you don't stop tearing up the room, I'll have to stop you. I think you've been battered enough for one day."

She heard it in his voice, the calm control, the half-amused exasperation. Despair for her abiding love merged with fury at his betrayal.

"Just leave me alone!"

"Lie down, B.J., and we'll talk later."

"No, don't you touch me," she ordered as he made to take her arm. "I mean it, Taylor, don't touch me!"

At the desperation in her voice, he dropped his hand to his side. "All right then." The first warning signals of anger touched his face. In the cool precision of his voice, she could hear the danger. "Suppose you tell me what exactly it is I've done?"

"You know very well."

"Spell it out for me," he interrupted, moving away and lighting a cigarette.

"That architect you brought here while we were in Florida."

"Fletcher?" Taylor cut her off again, but this time he gave her his full attention. "What about him?

"What about him?" B.J. repeated incredulously. "You brought him here behind my back, making all his little drawings and plans. You probably took me to Florida just to get me out of the way while he was here."

"That was a consideration."

His easy admission left her speechless. A wave of pain washed over her, reflecting in her eyes.

"B.J." Taylor's expression became more curious than angry. "Suppose you tell me precisely what you know."

"Darla was only too happy to enlighten me." Turning away, she assuaged the hurt with more furious packing. "Go talk to her."

"She's gone by now. I told her to leave. B.J., did you think I'd let her stay after she hit you?" The soft texture of his voice caused her hands to falter a moment. Quickly, she forced them to move again. "What did she say to you?"

"She told me everything. How you'd brought in the architect to draw up plans for turning the inn into a resort. That you're going to bring in someone to manage it, how . . ." Her voice broke. "It's bad enough you've been lying to me,

Taylor, bad enough you broke your word, but that's personal. What is more important is that you're going to change the whole structure of this community, alter dozens of lives for a few more dollars you don't even need. Your resort in Palm Beach is beautiful and perfect for where and what it is, but the inn . . ."

"Be quiet, B.J." He crushed out his cigarette then thrust his hands in his pockets. "I told you before, I make my own decisions. I called Fletcher in for two reasons." A swift gesture of his hand halted her furious retort. "One, to design a house for a piece of property my agent picked up for me last week. It's about ten miles outside of town, five acres on a hill overlooking the lake. You probably know it."

"Why do you need . . ."

"The second purpose," he continued, ignoring her, "was to design an addition to the inn, adhering to its present architecture. The office space is just too limited. Since I plan to move my base from New York to the inn after we're married, I require larger accommodations."

"I don't see . . ." Her words stumbled to a halt, as she stared into calm brown eyes. A medley of emotions played through her, eradicating the ache in her head. "I never agreed to marry you," she managed at length.

"But you will," he countered and leaned against her desk. "In the meantime, you can ease the various minds downstairs that the inn will remain as is, and you'll remain in the position of manager with some adjustments."

"Adjustments?" She could only parrot his last word and sink into a chair.

"I have no problem basing my business in Vermont, but I won't base my marriage in a hotel. Therefore, we'll live in the house when it's completed, and Eddie can take over some of your duties. You'll also have to be free to travel from time to time. We leave for Rome in three weeks."

"Rome?" she echoed him again, dimly remembering his speaking of Rome and passports.

"Yes, your mother's sending your birth certificate so you can see to getting a passport."

"My mother?" Unable to sit, B.J. rose and paced to the window, trying to clear the fog which covered her brain. "You seem to have everything worked out very neatly." She struggled for control. "I don't suppose it occurred to you to ask my feelings on the matter?"

"I know your feelings." His hands descended to her shoulders, and she stiffened. "I told you once, you can't keep secrets with those eyes."

"I guess it's very convenient for you that I happen to be in love with you." She swallowed, focusing on the gleam of the sun as it filtered through the pines on the hillside.

"It makes things less complicated." His fingers worked at the tension in her shoulders but she held herself rigid.

"Why do you want to marry me, Taylor?"

"Why do you think?" She felt his lips in her hair and squeezed her eyes shut.

"You don't have to marry me for that, and we both know it." Taking a deep breath, she gripped the windowsill tighter. "That first night you came to my room, you'd already won."

"It wasn't enough." His arms circled her waist and brought her back against him. She struggled to keep her mind clear. "The minute you swaggered into the office with invisible six guns at your hips, I made up my mind to marry you. I knew I could make you want me, I'd felt that the first time I held you, but the night in your room, you looked up at me, and I knew making you want me wasn't enough. I wanted you to love me."

"So"—she moved her shoulders as if it was of little consequence—"you comforted yourself with Darla in the meantime."

She was spun around so quickly, her hair flew out to fall over her face, obscuring vision. "I never touched Darla or anyone from the first minute I saw you. That little charade in the nightgown was strictly for your benefit, and you were stupid enough to fall for it. Do you think I could touch another woman when I had you on my mind?"

Without giving her time to answer, his mouth closed over hers, commanding and possessive. His arms banded her waist, dragging her against him. "You've been driving me crazy for nearly two weeks." Allowing her time to draw a quick breath, his mouth crushed hers again. Slowly, the kiss altered in texture, softening, sweetening, his hand moving with a tender lightness which drugged her reason.

"B.J.," he murmured, resting his chin on her hair. "It would be less intimidating if you owned a few more pounds and inches. I've had a devil of a time fighting my natural instincts. I don't want to hurt you, and you're much too small and much too innocent." Lifting her chin, he framed her face with his hands. "Have I told you yet that I love you?"

Her eyes grew wide, her mouth opening, but powerless to form sound. She shook her head briskly and swallowed the obstruction in her throat.

"I didn't think I had. Actually, I think I was hit the minute you stood up from home plate, turned those eyes on me and claimed you were absolutely safe." He bent down and brushed her lips.

She threw her arms around his neck as though he might vanish in a puff of smoke. "Taylor, why have you waited so long?"

Drawing her away, he lifted a brow in amusement, reminding her of the brevity of their relationship.

"It's been years," she claimed, burying her face in his shoulder as joy washed over her. "Decades, centuries."

"And during the millennium," he replied, stroking fingers through her hair, "you've been more exasperating than receptive. The day I came into the lounge and found you ticking off bourbon bottles, I had hoped to start things along a smooth road, but you turned on the ice very effectively. The next day in your room, when you switched to fire, it was very illuminating. The things you said made a great deal of sense, so I decided a change of setting and attitude were in order. Providentially, Bailey called from Florida."

"You said you had to go to Palm Beach to help him with a problem."

"I lied," he said simply, then laughed with great enjoyment at her astonishment. "I had planned," he began, dropping into a chair and pulling her into his lap, "to get you away from the inn for a couple of days. More important to have you to myself. I wanted you relaxed and perhaps a bit off guard." He laughed again and nuzzled her ear. "Of course, then I had to see you sitting with Hardy and looking like a fresh peach ripe for picking."

"You were jealous." Indescribably pleased, she sighed and burrowed closer.

"That's a mild word for it."

They spent the next few minutes in mutually agreeable silence. Taylor lingered over the taste of her mouth, his hand sliding beneath the barrier of her shirt. "I was quite determined to do things properly, hence the dinner and wine and soft music. I had fully intended to tell you I loved you and ask you to marry me that last night in Florida."

"Why didn't you?"

"You distracted me." His lips trailed along her cheek, reminding her of the power of their last night together. "I had no intention of allowing things to progress the way they did, but you have a habit of stretching my will power. That night it snapped. Then, I felt you trembling, and your eyes were so young." He sighed and rested his cheek on her hair. "I was furious with myself for losing control of the situation."

"I thought you were furious with me."

"It was better that you did. If I had told you then how I felt about you, nothing would have stopped me from taking you. I was in no frame of mind to introduce you gently to the ways of love. I've never needed anyone so much in my life as I needed you that night."

Round and liquid with love, her eyes lifted to his. "Do you need me, Taylor?"

His hand lifted to brush back her hair. The arm cradling her shifted her closer. "You look like a child," he murmured, tracing her lips with his finger. "A child's mouth, and I can't seem to do without the taste of it. Yes, B.J., I need you."

His mouth lowered, featherlight, but her arm circled his neck and demanded more. The pressure increased, and the door opened to the world of heat and passion. She felt his hand on her breast, never aware that the buttons of her shirt had been loosened. Her fingers tightened in his hair, willing him to prolong the ecstasy.

His mouth moved to her brow, then rested on her hair, his fingers tracing lightly over her bare skin. "You can see why I've been keeping away from you the last day or so."

With a soft sound of agreement, she buried her face against his shoulder.

"I wanted to get everything set up before I got near you again. I could have done with one more day; we still need a marriage license."

"I'll talk to Judge Walker," she murmured, "if you want one quickly. He's Eddie's uncle,"

"Small towns are the backbone of America," Taylor decided. He pulled her close to cover her mouth again when a frantic knock sounded on the door.

"B.J." Eddie's voice drifted through the panel. "Mrs. Frank wants to feed Julius, and I can't find his dinner. And the Bodwin sisters are out of sunflower seeds for Horatio."

"Who's Horatio?" Taylor demanded.

"The Bodwins' parakeet."

"Tell him to feed Horatio to Julius," he suggested, giving the door a scowl.

"It's a thought." Lingering on it briefly, B.J. cast it aside. "Julius's dinner is on the third shelf right hand side of the fridge," she called out. "Send someone into town for a package of sunflower seeds. Now, go away, Eddie, I'm very busy. Mr. Reynolds and I are in conference." With a smile, she circled Taylor's neck again. "Now, Mr. Reynolds, perhaps you'd like my views on the construction of this house you're planning as well as my educated opinion on the structure of your office space."

"Be quiet, B.J."

"You're the boss," she agreed the moment before their lips met.

Genuine Silhouette sterling silver bookmark for only $15.95!

What a beautiful way to hold your place in your current romance! This genuine sterling silver bookmark, with the distinctive Silhouette symbol in elegant black, measures 1½″ long and 1″ wide. It makes a beautiful gift for yourself, and for every romantic you know! And, at only $15.95 each, including all postage and handling charges, you'll want to order several now, while supplies last.

Send your name and address with check or money order for $15.95 per bookmark ordered to
Simon & Schuster Enterprises
120 Brighton Rd., P.O. Box 5020
Clifton, N.J. 07012
Attn: Bookmark

Bookmarks can be ordered pre-paid only. No charges will be accepted. Please allow 4-6 weeks for delivery.

N.Y. State Residents
Please Add Sales Tax

Silhouette Romance

IT'S YOUR OWN SPECIAL TIME

Contemporary romances for today's women.
Each month, six very special love stories will be yours
from SILHOUETTE. Look for them wherever books are sold
or order now from the coupon below.

$1.50 each

Hampson	☐ 1 ☐ 4 ☐ 16 ☐ 27 ☐ 28 ☐ 52 ☐ 94	Browning	☐ 12 ☐ 38 ☐ 53 ☐ 73 ☐ 93
Stanford	☐ 6 ☐ 25 ☐ 35 ☐ 46 ☐ 58 ☐ 88	Michaels	☐ 15 ☐ 32 ☐ 61 ☐ 87
		John	☐ 17 ☐ 34 ☐ 57 ☐ 85
Hastings	☐ 13 ☐ 26	Beckman	☐ 8 ☐ 37 ☐ 54 ☐ 96
Vitek	☐ 33 ☐ 47 ☐ 84	Wisdom	☐ 49 ☐ 95
Wildman	☐ 29 ☐ 48	Halston	☐ 62 ☐ 83

☐ 5 Goforth	☐ 22 Stephens	☐ 50 Scott	☐ 81 Roberts
☐ 7 Lewis	☐ 23 Edwards	☐ 55 Ladame	☐ 82 Dailey
☐ 9 Wilson	☐ 24 Healy	☐ 56 Trent	☐ 86 Adams
☐ 10 Caine	☐ 30 Dixon	☐ 59 Vernon	☐ 89 James
☐ 11 Vernon	☐ 31 Halldorson	☐ 60 Hill	☐ 90 Major
☐ 14 Oliver	☐ 36 McKay	☐ 63 Brent	☐ 92 McKay
☐ 19 Thornton	☐ 39 Sinclair	☐ 71 Ripy	☐ 97 Clay
☐ 20 Fulford	☐ 43 Robb	☐ 76 Hardy	☐ 98 St. George
☐ 21 Richards	☐ 45 Carroll	☐ 78 Oliver	☐ 99 Camp

$1.75 each

Stanford	☐ 100 ☐ 112 ☐ 131	Browning	☐ 113 ☐ 142 ☐ 164 ☐ 172
Hardy	☐ 101 ☐ 130 ☐ 184	Michaels	☐ 114 ☐ 146
Cork	☐ 103 ☐ 148 ☐ 188	Beckman	☐ 124 ☐ 154 ☐ 179
Vitek	☐ 104 ☐ 139 ☐ 157 ☐ 176	Roberts	☐ 127 ☐ 143 ☐ 163 ☐ 180
Dailey	☐ 106 ☐ 118 ☐ 153 ☐ 177	Trent	☐ 110 ☐ 161
Bright	☐ 107 ☐ 125	Wisdom	☐ 132 ☐ 166
Hampson	☐ 108 ☐ 119 ☐ 128 ☐ 136 ☐ 147 ☐ 151 ☐ 155 ☐ 160 ☐ 178 ☐ 185	Hunter	☐ 137 ☐ 167
		Scott	☐ 117 ☐ 169 ☐ 187
		Sinclair	☐ 123 ☐ 174

Coming next month from
Silhouette Romances

Dreamtime by Anne Hampson

When Jane left America for the Australian Outback she had high hopes for a happy new life. But there she met domineering Scott Farnham and found herself in a heartbreaking trap.

A Secret Valentine by Dixie Browning

Now that Grace Spencer's life was finally well-ordered and sensible, she didn't need construction worker Quinn Donovan breaking down old walls and building up new expectations in her heart!

Midnight Sun by Mary Carroll

When Tag Hansen's car ran into Lark, she thought it was the end of her holiday . . . until he extended his hospitality and had Lark rearrange all her plans.

Race the Tide by Mia Maxam

Deceiving Scott Kirkner in her mechanics coveralls was fun . . . until Christina fell in love. How could she tell Scott his mechanic was the same beautiful woman he had romanced?

An Adventure In Love by Marilyn Manning

While in London Julie Brewster had agreed to stay with Morgan Stuart, an old friend of her grandfathers'. But Morgan was young and attractive and Julie fell passionately in love!

More Precious Than Pearls by Susannah Windham

When Manzanillo Arismendi grudgingly offered advertising executive Leeanne Mullins his prestigious account, she knew she could handle it—but handling Manzanillo was altogether another matter.

Silhouette Desire
15-Day Trial Offer

A new romance series
that explores
contemporary relationships
in exciting detail

Six Silhouette Desire romances, free for 15 days!
We'll send you six new Silhouette Desire romances
to look over for 15 days, absolutely free! If you decide
not to keep the books, return them and owe nothing.

Six books a month, free home delivery. If you like
Silhouette Desire romances as much as we think you
will, keep them and return your payment with the
invoice. Then we will send you six new books every
month to preview, just as soon as they are published.
You pay only for the books you decide to keep, and
you never pay postage and handling.

READERS' COMMENTS ON SILHOUETTE ROMANCES:

"I would like to congratulate you on the most wonderful books I've had the pleasure of reading. They are a tremendous joy to those of us who have yet to meet the man of our dreams. From reading your books I quite truly believe that he will some-day appear before me like a prince!"

—L.L.*, Hollandale, MS

"Your books are great, wholesome fiction, always with an upbeat, happy ending. Thank you."

—M.D., Massena, NY

"My boyfriend always teases me about Silhouette Books. He asks me, how's my love life and natu-rally I say terrific, but I tell him that there is always room for a little more romance from Sil-houette."

—F.N., Ontario, Canada

"I would like to sincerely express my gratitude to you and your staff for bringing the pleasure of your publications to my attention. Your books are well written, mature and very contemporary."

—D.D., Staten Island, NY

*names available on request